KU-090-416

0709 080565 2524 49

Sharpshooters and the Rainman

McGee and Salmon, two circus sharpshooters, find their lives are lacking excitement in the small town of Stoneville that has been hit by a drought. Their boredom is relieved when Salmon saves the life of a beautiful Indian squaw named Tandolee.

Explaining how she and her father – nicknamed the Rainman – used to predict the coming of the rain, McGee sees an easy way of making money. But a gang of outlaws is also scheming to take advantage of the drought.

With Tandolee in danger, McGee and Salmon clash with the outlaws and test their sharpshooting skills to the extreme.

Sharpshooters and the Rainman

Ron Watkins

A Black Horse Western

ROBERT HALE · LONDON

© Ron Watkins 2006
First published in Great Britain 2006

ISBN-10: 0-7090-8056-5
ISBN-13: 978-0-7090-8056-5

Robert Hale Limited
Clerkenwell House
Clerkenwell Green
London EC1R 0HT

The right of Ron Watkins to be identified as
author of this work has been asserted by him
in accordance with the Copyright, Designs and
Patents Act 1988.

WOLVERHAMPTON LIBRARIES	
0709080565252449	
HJ	434086
	£10.99
SV ΛAUS	

Typeset by
Derek Doyle & Associates, Shaw Heath
Printed and bound in Great Britain by
Antony Rowe Limited, Wiltshire

For my granddaughter, Jessica Watkins

CHAPTER 1

McGee stared up at the endless blue sky above him. He was relaxing on the short brown grass with his hands behind his neck.

'You know I could easily get used to this way of life,' he said.

Salmon, his companion, who was stretched out a few feet away replied: 'We should be getting used to it by now. How many weeks is it since we've had nothing to do?'

'Who's counting?' McGee replied, airily.

'It's at least a month,' Salmon persisted. 'A month just lying around here with nothing to do. And Jill and Letitia away in New York.'

'They're probably enjoying themselves, too,' said McGee, dismissively. The two ladies mentioned were their wives. Their intended visit to New York the previous year had been

7

cancelled by an outbreak of smallpox which had forced them to stay with their husbands in the small town of Stoneville. But a few weeks before they had learned that New York was now clear of the infectious disease. So they had set out with their offspring to visit their parents and display their respective children.

'How much longer do you think this will go on?' demanded Salmon.

'Who cares?' replied McGee.

'The other cowboys are saying they've never known anything like it.' Salmon stretched his long frame out further. He was a big man while McGee would be described as short and wiry, and also a ladies' man. Before his marriage he had been very successful in the amorous field – especially with certain types of ladies.

McGee squinted up at the afternoon sun. He adjusted his Stetson to avoid the glare.

'There's only one thing wrong with this life.'

'What's that?' demanded Salmon.

'We haven't any money. We've given all the money we had to Letitia and Jill to go to New York.'

'If we had money there's no place to spend it in this one-horse town,' retorted Salmon.

'There are the saloons.'

'All two of them. And anyhow you're not

allowed in them because you've cleaned out the regulars by playing poker so many times that they've threatened to walk out if you go in there.'

'They're only country hicks,' said McGee, dismissively. 'They won't believe me when I tell them that when I was in New York I put as much as a thousand dollars in the pot on one hand of poker.'

'And lost it if I remember rightly.'

'Yeah. But it was worth it.' McGee began to roll a cigarette. 'Maybe we should have gone to New York with our wives. It's better than rotting alive in this place.'

'Ten minutes ago you said it was the perfect place to be.'

'Yes, but think of all those card-schools in New York.'

'And think of Charlie the Hook.'

The mention of the name brought McGee's brief flight of fancy to an abrupt end. It had been McGee's prediliction for gambling which had forced them to leave New York in a hurry a year before. Their exit had been due to the fact that McGee owed a gang-leader named Charlie the Hook $5,000 in gambling debts. Charlie the Hook was not the type of person who took kindly to being owed such a large sum of money when there was no evidence of any immediate repayment. His advice had been succinct but it had been no less threatening for that.

'If I don't have the money by the end of the week, they'll find another body in the Hudson river. Yours.'

McGee and Salmon adopted the only course that was open to them – they jumped on the next train out of the city. Their aim was to put the longest distance possible between themselves and Charlie the Hook and his gang. That was why they had settled in the remote town of Stoneville.

'The horses need water,' said Salmon. 'We might as well take them down to the river.'

The river was the town's main source of water. In view of the drought it would be supposed that the river level would be exceptionally low. However, due to the fact that the river was supplied from several springs up in the mountains the river had more or less maintained its usual level.

'Yes, I suppose we'd better water them,' McGee concurred.

Ten minutes later, having saddled their horses, they were riding towards Stoneville.

'Maybe we could have a swim in the river,' suggested Salmon.

'I didn't like to mention it, but it would be a very good idea if you were to have a dip in the river.'

'What do you mean?'

'You're beginning to smell. If Jill were here now, she'd have given you a bar of soap and told you to get down to the river.'

'You're not exactly smelling of roses yourself,' retorted Salmon.

When they neared Stoneville they could see the river in the distance. It was obvious that the horses, too, had become aware that they were heading for water, since they quickened their pace without being given the rein by their riders. There was quite a large crowd by the river and the two headed towards it, without being sure why so many people were congregated. They knew that sometimes the river was used for a baptism, but that was invariably on a Sunday, and today was Tuesday. Also when there was a baptism the crowd would be singing one of their hymns, such as 'We'll All Gather At The River'. But this crowd weren't singing. In fact everybody seemed to be excited about something, judging from the way they were shouting.

When McGee and Salmon were near enough to see what was happening, they both took in the scene with stunned surprise. The crowd were

11

cheering because they were carrying out an ancient punishment; a punishment which some said went back hundreds of years. The crowd were subjecting some poor soul to the ancient punishment of ducking, using the old instrument specially constructed for the purpose – a ducking-stool.

CHAPTER 2

The duo drew up their horses a short distance from the river. They tied them to a convenient tree – much to the disgust of the animals who snorted to show their displeasure.

'You can go in the river later,' Salmon promised his brown-and-white mare.

'Oh, come on,' said McGee, impatiently, as he headed for the river.

Salmon followed close behind.

The ducking-stool consisted of a long thick pole about two feet in diameter. It was about twelve feet in length and at its end was a familiar shape which resembled a chair in which young children were put to make sure they stayed in one place and kept out of mischief. It had arms to prevent the occupant from falling out. But the main difference between this and a child's armchair was the straps which were designed to hold the occupant firmly in place.

The ducking-stool at the other end had an iron handle which, when turned, controlled the movements of the ducking stool – making it go up or down as needed. There were also two large iron wheels which allowed the contraption to be moved into the river in the first place. The ducking-stool's usual place of residence was the church. It fitted neatly along one of the aisles and on the few occasions when their wives had forcibly persuaded Salmon and McGee to go to church, they had been vaguely aware of its existence. If questioned they would have expressed the opinion that the ducking-stool was there as a warning to wrongdoers. As far as they knew it hadn't been used for years. But now here it was, having been trundled out of the church and down the slope to the river.

The crowd expressed their satisfaction with a cheer as the unfortunate occupant of the stool was ducked once more. Salmon and McGee, who had joined the crowd, watched the bedraggled female form as she was held under water. They could see her struggling ineffectively against the thongs that held her.

'What's she done?' Salmon asked a man who standing nearby. The man's reply took the duo by surprise.

'She's a witch.'

'Don't be stupid,' said McGee. 'There haven't been witches for over two hundred years.'

'Not in our civilization. But it's different with the Indians.' The wretched figure was now pulled up out of the water and it was obvious that she was indeed an Indian.

'So what's she done?' persisted Salmon.

'She's put a spell on Farmer Guerney's cattle. They haven't produced any milk for weeks.'

'That's because there's been a drought.' McGee, who had dragged his gaze away from the fetching sight of the Indian whose dress now fitted her like a mermaid's skin, gave his opinion.

'She said she was going to put a spell on Guerney's cattle and she did,' said the man, stubbornly.

'Nobody in their right senses would believe a stupid thing like that.'

'Are you calling me stupid?' The man had adopted a belligerent stance. Salmon was aware that he wore guns, which was rather unusual in this peaceful community. McGee, on the other hand, wasn't carrying a gun. As if to emphasize the point that he was armed the man's right hand took up a threatening position a few inches above the gun.

Salmon, who had been standing to the man's left, imperceptibly moved nearer to him. McGee also moved slightly – he was now standing facing the man but a few feet away.

'You had better apologize,' snapped the man, whose name was Grimson, in a tone of voice which announced conclusively that he held all the aces.

'I don't see why I should.'

McGee's reply caused Grimson's lips to tighten and his hand inch towards his gun.

The section of the crowd around McGee and Salmon, sensing a conflict which could have a more interesting result than the event in the river, turned their full attention on the drama that was unfolding. They also moved back in order to give the combatants more space.

'If I drew my gun I could shoot off one of your toes.'

If the man thought the threat would cause McGee to change his mind and apologize he was rather taken aback by the reaction. McGee smiled broadly. If the man had turned his head to glance at Salmon he would have seen a similar wide smile on Salmon's face.

'I'm giving you one more chance to apologize.'

'Why don't you go back home.'

16

The remark turned the man's face, which had sported a crimson hue, into something resembling a deep purple. His hand moved deliberately towards his gun. To the onlookers, many of whom had lived in the West for years, the threat was obvious.

'I wouldn't draw if I were you.'

McGee's remark for a moment halted the progress of Grimson's hand. He stared at McGee in disbelief. Here he was, within an inch of drawing his gun, and the guy opposite was telling him not to go ahead. If he had been imploring him not to draw, then he could have understood it. But to have the gall to stand there and defy him was beyond belief.

They stood facing each other as still as gravestones. Grimson knew that the next move was up to him. If he backed down then he would lose face. Many of the onlookers would recognize him, particularly in a small town like Stoneville, where most of the people knew each other. He had no choice but to draw and put a bullet as near to McGee's toes as possible. Yes, he would make him jump. He would wipe the smile off his face.

It was McGee though who made the next move. He unfolded his arms and let them drop casually by his side. Grimson's eyes narrowed.

McGee, who had been in dozens of similar situations, recognized the immediate threat. What happened next was such a blur of movement that many of the onlookers didn't see the sequence of events until they saw their conclusion. Salmon reached across and whipped out Grimson's gun from his holster. He tossed the revolver to McGee who caught it adroitly and spun it in his hand. Grimson's other gun had barely cleared its holster when he realized he was facing his own gun which was in McGee's hand. He was also facing an entirely different person from the smiling cowboy he had faced a few seconds before. This person's face was now set in hard lines.

'I believe you said something about shooting toes off,' snapped McGee. He pointed the revolver at Grimson's foot and fired. The bullet went near to Grimson's foot. Grimson involuntarily jumped back.

'Throw your other gun on the floor.'

Grimson obeyed with alacrity.

'I'll be dropping these into the sheriff's office. No doubt he'll have something to say to a person who is carrying guns in a peaceful town event. Now get out of my sight before I really shoot your toe off.'

'He could, too,' Salmon confirmed.

Grimson scuttled off, barging his way unceremoniously through the crowd. A few of the onlookers who were standing nearby moved forward to congratulate McGee.

'He's a pig of a man,' said one. 'It's great to see him taken down a peg.'

At that moment there was a shout from that part of the crowd who had been watching the ducking in the river. The tone of the shout wasn't that of onlookers who had been enjoying the discomfort of the young Indian who was being ducked in the river. This was a cry of horror.

CHAPTER 3

The horror with which the scene on the river had made the crowd gasp had not been exaggerated. While McGee and Salmon had been concentrating on disarming the gunman, the action involving the ducking-stool had taken an unexpected and potentially tragic turn. Instead of the stool rising and descending into the river with monotonous regularity, taking with it its unfortunate occupant, it was as if the contraption had decided to take on a life of its own. The first the two men who had been operating the machine knew about any change was when the ducking stool suddenly moved further into the river. This in itself was not alarming – the two men obediently moved with it. The one who was turning the handle now found himself up to his chest in water, whereas previously he had been only up to his waist. But he was still able to turn the handle, even though it was more of an effort. Similarly his companion, whose task had been to hold the machine steady while the stool performed its regular movement, was forced to move into deeper water. Neither of them however had foreseen what was going to happen next. It was the ducking-stool's next move that brought the gasp of horror from the onlookers. It suddenly toppled on to its side.

There was no way that the Indian could escape. She was securely tied with thongs that had been tightened to give her the minimum of movement. The first thought of the two who had been operating the ducking-stool was that they needed a knife to cut the throngs before the stool's occupant drowned. Unfortunately, since they were both stripped to the waist, it was obvious that neither of them carried a knife. While they regarded each other as the full horror of the situation dawned on them, a figure shot past them. Salmon, for one so big, had covered the intervening distance to the river in record time.

Salmon grasped one of the iron wheels. As a strong-man in the circus he had performed several feats of strength including tying a knot in an iron bar, but here the problem was different. He not only had the weight of the ducking-stool to contend with, but also the fact that the weight

21

of the water was added to it. The crowd held its breath as Salmon strained to turn the ducking stool back to its upright position. They could see his powerful muscles tightening as he struggled with the stubborn wheel. Every second that passed while he failed to restore the contraption back on an even keel meant that they were added to the chances of the stool's occupant of being a victim of death by drowning. She was already half-drowned before the ducking-stool had toppled over and now her chances of survival were ebbing away with every second that passed.

Salmon gave one last desperate heave. The river responded with a curious sucking noise as it reluctantly relinquished its hold on the ducking-stool. The onlookers gave a loud cheer as they saw the results of Salmon's efforts in the machine being restored to its upright position. The Indian, like a bedraggled doll, was now out of the water. McGee had materialized by her side. He cut the thongs holding her arms. Her eyes were closed and judging by the small bubbles of water coming from her lips it appeared that Salmon's efforts to save her had been too late.

Salmon carried her to the river-bank. The crowd parted reverently to give him room. He laid her face down on a dry spot. He began rhythmically to press her back.

After a dozen or so efforts it seemed that Salmon's attempt at saving her had been in vain. Indeed a few of the onlookers voiced the opinion that she was already dead.

McGee swung on them, his face twisted with anger.

'If she's dead, then all of you are responsible for her death,' he snarled.

'It wasn't our fault,' piped up one. 'She was responsible for the drought. Her father was a witchdoctor.'

'I've never heard such rubbish in my life,' snapped McGee. 'You've killed this poor Indian because of your bigoted beliefs.'

'She's a savage,' stated one of the crowd.

'She's not a savage. You're the ones who are savages.' McGee was shouting now. 'I always thought that the West was a place where people could start a new life with hope and dignity. What you've shown here is that you are all still living in the dark ages when your ancestors believed in witchcraft.'

Any further outbursts from McGee were interrupted by a shout from Salmon. 'I think she's coming round.'

It was true. The rhythmical pressure which

Salmon had applied to her back had had its desired effect. The Indian was now coughing and spluttering out water. In fact it seemed as though she must have swallowed gallons of the stuff since her retching went on and on.

'You'll be all right now,' said Salmon, as he continued to apply pressure to her back to make sure that she coughed up all the water.

After what seemed like an eternity later but was probably only a few minutes, she was able to sit up. She pushed her hair away from her face which had effectively hidden her features. She revealed an attractive young face.

'He saved your life.' McGee indicated Salmon.

'Is that true?' she regarded Salmon with large brown eyes.

'I managed to turn the ducking-stool back. It had fallen on its side and you were trapped underneath.'

Her gaze never left his face. 'I didn't know what happened. All I knew was that I was drowning. I think I had a bump on the head.'

'You probably hit your head on a stone when the ducking-stool fell over,' said McGee.

'You must be very strong to be able to turn it upright.'

'He was a strong-man in a circus,' supplied McGee.

Salmon was finding the discussion more than a little embarrassing. 'Well you've recovered now, that's the main thing.'

'Thanks to you. It means I am indebted to you for life.' Her eyes were fixed on Salmon's face as though she was trying to read something there.

'I just happened to be in the right place at the right time.' Salmon moved as though to stand up.

She grasped his hand to restrain him. 'You don't understand. I'm a Crow Indian and one of our creeds is that if someone saves your life, you belong to that person.'

McGee grasped the significance of her remark more quickly than Salmon. 'You mean you will become his squaw?'

'Exactly.' She flashed McGee a smile in acknowledgement of his grasp of the situation.

'But I'm already married.' The statement came out louder than Salmon had intended and some of the onlookers regarded him with sudden interest.

'We'd better discuss this somewhere quiet,' said McGee, diplomatically.

CHAPTER 4

Ten minutes later Salmon and McGee were seated in the front room of a cottage belonging to a Miss Brown. She was a middle-aged spinster who had introduced herself to them while the Indian, whose name they had discovered was Tandolee was recovering from her ordeal on the river's edge.

'If the girl stands around much longer in those wet clothes she'll die of pneumonia,' she informed Salmon and McGee. 'You'd better bring her to my house where she can dry out, and I'll find some tidy clothes for her.'

Many of the men who were standing around had been casting admiring glances at the Indian's shapely figure which her skimpy wet clothes did nothing to hide. Salmon, who somehow felt that he was responsible for Tandolee's complete recovery, agreed with alacrity.

'I know you think we are all savages here,' said Miss Brown, as she led the way to her cottage. 'But perhaps I can show you that at least some of us are not devoid of the milk of human kindness.'

McGee had the grace to blush. 'I'm sorry, but it was all said in a moment of anger.'

'Yes, well maybe part of it is true,' she concurred.

They presented a strange sight as the progressed down the Main Street; Miss Brown was smartly dressed in clothes she might have been wearing to go to church, Salmon and McGee were in their shirts and jeans and Tandolee, who was dripping water at every step. Salmon too had become soaked due to the episode in the river and he was also uncomfortably aware of his clothes clinging to him as he walked along, with Tandolee hung on to his arm.

Miss Brown brought in a couple of cups of coffee. 'I've found some clothes for Tandolee,' she announced. 'They belong to my niece who sometimes comes to stay with me.'

When Tandolee eventually entered the room, the duo were surprised at the transformation in her appearance. She was wearing a frilly blouse and crinoline skirt which any young lady in the town might have worn. Her long, unruly hair had been combed and was tied with a ribbon. Indeed the only difference in her attire was that she was not wearing shoes.

'You look very smart,' said McGee.

She pointedly ignored him and went over to sit at Salmon's feet.

'I'll fetch you a cup of coffee, my dear,' said Miss Brown.

'Is there somewhere where I can dry out?' demanded Salmon.

'There's a fire in the kitchen. You are welcome to stand in front of it to help you to dry out. I'm afraid I haven't any spare clothes to give you. There haven't been any menfolk in this house for many years.'

When they were left alone in the room McGee asked: 'Why did the townsfolk accuse you of causing the drought?'

'Because my father was a witchdoctor. And because they wanted to blame somebody for the things which have been happening during the drought.'

'So they picked on you?'

'That's right. Since my skin isn't the same colour as most of the people of the town, I was an obvious target.' She was studying her feet as though seeing them for the first time.

'It doesn't seem much of a reason for putting

you in the ducking-stool.'

'The other reason was that they expected me to make it rain. But I couldn't.'

'Your father is what the Indians call a Rain Man?'

'He was. He died a few months ago.'

'I'm sorry. Did he really believe he could bring rain?'

'Oh, yes. We did it quite a few times.'

'We?'

'I used to help him.'

'I don't understand.'

'I don't suppose there's any harm in telling you. Since you and Salmon are friends.'

'We're like blood-brothers,' said McGee, piously.

'The rain always comes from the west, right?'

'Yes.'

'So I would go up to the top of the mountain. Then when I could see the rain clouds gathering I would give him a signal.'

The surprise on McGee's face was almost comical to see. Eventually he said: 'How did you send him a signal?'

'How do you think? By a smoke signal, of course.'

Salmon and Miss Brown returned. She handed Tandolee a cup of coffee.

'Have you thought what's going to happen to you now?' she asked.

'She'll be all right,' said McGee quickly. 'Salmon and I will see that she comes to no harm. We're both married men and we can guarantee that she'll be safe.'

'Well I wouldn't let her wander around in the town, if I were you. There are some unpleasant characters hanging around the town these days. If they saw Tandolee they might decide that they have some unfinished business to attend to.'

Tandolee finished her coffee. 'Thank you for the coffee.'

'It was nothing, my dear. And you can keep the clothes you are wearing. I don't think my niece will want them again.'

When they were out in the street, Salmon asked: 'What are we going to do with Tandolee?'

'I'm coming with you,' she said, as she happily skipped along by Salmon's side.

'But you heard what McGee said – we're married,' protested Salmon.

'It doesn't matter. I'm your servant now for life. If you don't want to sleep with me, I can cook, hunt and skin animals and mend clothes.'

'And you can watch out for rain clouds,' put in McGee.

'What are you talking about?' demanded Salmon.

'Tell him about what you told me about your father,' prompted McGee.

Tandolee explained how they used to fool the townsfolk by pretending that they could bring rain.

'That was a good trick,' said Salmon, appreciatively.

'Did you make much money out of it?' asked McGee,

'Oh, yes. Several hundred dollars. Of course it all went to my brother when my father died.'

'Several hundred dollars,' said McGee, thoughtfully.

Salmon who had been McGee's friend for several years and knew exactly what he was thinking when money was involved said emphatically: 'Oh, no.'

'Think of it,' said McGee, enthusiastically. 'You and Tandolee could go to the top of the mountain. I'd watch you from here. When the rain clouds began to appear Tandolee could give a smoke signal. I'd persuade the locals that rain was on its way. They could bet me that it wasn't. I would be sure to win. And the town would have rain and everybody would be happy.'

'I think it's a great idea,' beamed Tandolee.

31

'Salmon and I could start on our way up the mountain now before it gets too dark.'

'We'll go back to the ranch first to get some blankets for you,' stated McGee.

'I wouldn't bother too much about blankets,' said Tandolee. 'I'll keep Salmon warm.'

They had reached the spot where they had tethered their horses. 'That's what I'm afraid of,' said Salmon to himself, as he untied his horse.

CHAPTER 5

A few days later there was a meeting in the town to discuss the drought. There were three people present: the sheriff, who was a middle-aged man named Moody, the doctor, named Brand, who was about the same age as the sheriff, and the preacher, a younger man named Tindall.

The three, as the chief citizens of the town, often met in the sheriff's office to discuss any matters of common interest in the running of the town. Their topics for discussion had varied during the past year or so and had included the possibility of the railroad coming to the town (which hadn't materialized), the possibility of a large hotel being built in the town (which also hadn't materialized), the possibility of providing an extra classroom for the town's children (which had materialized) and now, by far the most important topic they had discussed – the drought.

'How long has it being going on now?' asked the doctor.

'I make it just over three months,' said Tindall.

'In all the sixteen years I've been a sheriff, I've never known anything like it,' said Moody.

'It's not only the lack of water, it's the threat of disease,' said the doctor.

'Before the drought started there were thirty-two wells serving the town,' said the sheriff. 'I've sent my deputy round the town to count how many of them have run dry. Do you know how many?'

'Sixteen. We've only got half the wells we normally have. That means extra people are using them. It's got to the situation where there is one closing almost every day.'

'The danger is that the farmers are bringing their cattle here to the river so that they can have something to drink,' said the doctor.

'It's the only way some of them can keep their cattle alive,' said the sheriff. 'They haven't got any grazing-grass left.'

'Yes, but it means that the river has become polluted with the excrement from the cattle.'

'I'll put some notices around telling the

townsfolk they should only drink water from the wells,' said the sheriff.

'I'll drive the point home when I hold my service on Sunday,' said Tindall.

'Perhaps you can also help by praying for rain,' suggested the doctor.

'The drought has also meant that there are a lot of cowboys hanging around the town,' said the sheriff quickly, on seeing that the doctor's last remark hadn't been too well received by the preacher. 'Normally they would be working on their ranches, but since nothing is happening there, a lot of them are spending their time in the town. The unfortunate thing is that some of them are looking for trouble.'

'It will get back to normal when the rain comes,' stated the doctor. 'But make sure you put those notices up.'

'I even let the townsfolk go ahead with ducking the Indian to let them have some free entertainment, but of course it almost ended in tragedy.'

'What happened?' demanded the doctor. 'I was out of town at the time, delivering a baby in a remote farm.'

The sheriff explained about Tandolee's ducking and how it would have ended in tragedy if a cowboy hadn't pulled her out of the water.

'Some of the townsfolk claimed that she was a witch,' put in the preacher.

'Surely they couldn't have been serious. Witchcraft went out in Salem a couple of hundred years ago.'

'It's all a part of the devil's work,' said the preacher, piously.

'Poppycock. There aren't any witches around, just as there isn't any evidence that a devil exists.'

'Perhaps you should come to my service next Sunday and find out the truth about the devil and evil,' said the preacher, who was beginning to get angry.

'I think we'll draw this meeting to an end,' said the sheriff, diplomatically. 'We'll meet the same time next week when we can but hope that the rain will have come by then.'

'Amen,' said the preacher.

McGee too was wondering when the rain would come. Salmon and Tandolee had been up the mountain now for seven days and there had been no sign of any smoke signals to announce the imminent arrival of rain. McGee was bored with looking up at the top of the mountain at regular intervals to see if there was going to be a change from the persistent sunshine. It started shortly after the sky lightened in the early morning and went on until the red orb had descended below the horizon at night.

Since there was no work at the ranch. McGee was spending his time in town. This suited him since he realized that when he eventually saw the smoke signal he would have to move quickly. He had prepared the ground carefully during the past week. It was essential for him to become known among the townsfolk as a gambler. While most of the cowboys on the ranch where he worked could vouch for his claim to be one – as the number of times they had lost at cards to McGee would be sufficient evidence – to the men in the town he was just another cowboy, although some of them had seen the speed with which he could draw a gun.

In order to establish himself as a gambler McGee joined in as many card-schools as possible. He usually managed to win. Although they were small amounts, they all contributed to his ultimate plan. By joining in the card-schools he had now collected the sum of thirty dollars. He wished it could have been more, but if he could receive some good odds on the rain coming then that thirty dollars would increase quickly into a considerably larger amount.

CHAPTER 6

Salmon, too, up on the mountain was wondering when the rain would finally come. Not that Tandolee was an uninteresting companion – indeed if he could have picked a female with whom to spend several days on the mountain (apart from his beloved Jill, of course) he could not have had better company. For one thing they always had enough food to eat – and this to Salmon, who was a big man, was an essential ingredient for happiness. True, the food consisted largely of rabbit, of which species there was an abundance on the top of the mountain, but Tandolee was always ready to provide him with a meal whenever he wanted one.

The number of rabbits they had killed could be counted by the heap of skins which were lying on ground. When the rabbit had been shot Tandolee insisted on skinning it carefully and drying it. 'Where I come from these skins are valuable,' she informed Salmon. 'When I get enough I can make a blanket out of them.'

'It's easier to buy a blanket from the store,' said Salmon.

'You do not understand.' For the first time during their acquaintance she became angry. 'Most of the time we Indians are hungry. We are used to that – it is a part of our way of life. But the other thing we have to fear is the cold – it gets very cold on the reservation in the winter – so we save all the skins we can get. Then we make them into blankets for the old folk.'

'I'm sorry,' said Salmon, contritely. 'As you say, I don't understand.'

She smiled at him. 'No, it's all a different world from yours.'

A considerable amount of their time was spent in teaching Tandolee to shoot. In the beginning it was Salmon who shot the rabbits. On the second day, however, Tandolee asked: 'Can I try shooting one?'

'Have you ever used a revolver before?' asked Salmon.

'No,' she confessed.

Salmon showed her how to hold it. 'You hold it steady and take careful aim.'

'I can shoot a bow and arrow. I shouldn't have

any difficulty in holding it steady.'

Indeed Tandolee proved to be a willing and excellent pupil. She was soon shooting rabbits at a range of over a hundred yards.

'If I had a rifle I could shoot them at three times the distance,' she announced.

Salmon smiled at her enthusiasm. 'I expect you could.'

'Who's the best shot? You or McGee?'

'Oh, McGee easily. He can hit a coin if you flip it up in the air.'

She thought for a moment. Then she said: 'Have you got a coin?'

'No. And you're certainly not going to waste any bullets by shooting at one. We want all the bullets we've got to keep us in food.'

She pretended to pout. But by now they had got used to each other's ways and Salmon knew that she wasn't serious.

The other thing on which they spent considerable time was in building the fire, to be used when the rain clouds appeared. Since they were on the top of the mountain trees were very sparse and there was very little brushwood around. This meant that while one stayed in their makeshift camp the other went off in search of something which could burn. On one occasion when Salmon was in the camp, while

Tandolee was out looking for wood, he was surprised to hear the sound of a shot. Although they had agreed that one of them should always stay in the camp Salmon ignored this and rushed in the direction from where the shot had come. He found Tandolee in a clearing. To his surprise she seemed to be doing an Indian dance. Although she was aware of his presence she carried on for a few moments with her dance. She held her arms about her head and moved to some imaginary music. Her movements were graceful and it seemed to Salmon, who had seen many dancers in New York, that she would have held an audience enthralled, just as his gaze was riveted to her. In fact he was concentrating so much on her movements that it took a little time to realize the cause of her dance. As she moved in one of the intricate patterns she pointed to something lying on the far side of the clearing. Salmon went over to examine it. He saw a small wild pig with a neat bullet hole in its head.

'I shot him in the head.' Tandolee finished her dance and joined Salmon to examine the pig. 'He was running like the wind but I got him in the head. You know what this means?'

Salmon smiled at her enthusiasm. 'It means you've become a good shot.'

CHAPTER 7

In the town the lawlessness which the sheriff had feared had become more threatening daily. The cowboys from the two largest spreads, the Double L and the Circle T had been itching for a confrontation for weeks. There were several dozen of them from each ranch and while to begin with their confrontation had been largely confined to taunts, they had now reached the stage where the verbal abuse had become translated into physical violence. There were now fights almost every hour. While these were confined to fists the sheriff knew that they were comparably harmless activities. In fact they helped the cowboys to let off steam. And in that respect they might even be considered a good thing. But the danger that the sheriff foresaw was that at some point somebody would draw a gun. And from that moment the town could degenerate into lawlessness.

He and his deputy were seated outside their office. From their vantage point, since they were about half-way along Main Street, they could see almost the whole length of the street.

'There seem to be more fights now,' observed the deputy, a young man named Briers whose ambition was to become the sheriff when his boss retired in a few years' time.

'It's not the fist-fights I'm worried about.' The sheriff lit a cigar, which was a regular habit of his at this time in the afternoon.

'So far there haven't been any gunfights,' observed Briers. 'If there had been, we would have heard them.'

'It's only a matter of time. Unless of course the rain comes first.'

'It's been eighty-six days now. I've marked it off on the calendar.'

It was shortly afterwards when they heard the shot. It came from Main Street.

'It could have come from the Wind and Whistle saloon,' suggested Briers.

'Wherever it came from we've got to find the culprit,' said the sheriff.

They went into the room at the back of the office where they kept the guns. They fastened their gunbelts in silence. Their grim faces showed that they were not eagerly anticipating their meeting with whoever had fired the shot.

The cause of the disturbance was in fact a Circle T cowboy named Sankey. At that moment he was standing at the bar of the Wind and Whistle saloon. In fact he was standing at the centre of the bar on his own – anyone who had happened to be near him having instantly moved several yards away when he had fired the shot into the ceiling.

He was talking, or rather shouting at another cowboy who was at the far end of the bar. This cowboy was pointedly trying to ignore him.

'Hey! I'm talking to you.' Sankey hurled the words at the other figure.

The couple of dozen men who were in the bar watched the impending confrontation with interest. It did not escape their notice that while Sankey was holding a revolver, the person he was addressing was unarmed.

'When I talk to somebody I expect them to look me in the eye,' said Sankey.

There was no reply from the other. Everyone was still. The barman, who was also frozen to the spot, spoke up.

'You don't want to start any trouble, do you, Charlie?'

'If there is any trouble, he'd be the one who

started it. They all say that he's the fastest gun in town. Well, let him prove it.'

The so-called fastest gun, who turned out to be none other than McGee, swung round to give Charlie his full attention.

'You can put that gun away and I'll buy you a drink,' said McGee, pleasantly.

'I wouldn't drink with you, if you were the last man on earth,' snarled Charlie. 'You've been cheating at cards and you deserve what's coming to you.'

'You're talking nonsense. I haven't been cheating at cards.'

'Oh, no?' sneered Charlie. 'If you haven't been cheating, how is it that you've been winning at every card-game you've played in?' There was a murmur of agreement from several of the onlookers who had also been on the losing end at McGee's card-tables.

'It's just that I'm a good player.'

'You've taken all my pay for the last few weeks.' Charlie waved his revolver in the air to emphasize his point. McGee's eyes followed it warily.

'If you play cards you can expect to lose.'

McGee realized that he had said the wrong thing when Charlie sent a bullet a few inches above his head. There was a collective gasp of horror from the onlookers when they realised how close the bullet had been. The only one who seemed unperturbed by the shot was McGee, who still stood calmly facing Charlie.

The shot had brought a response from the barman. He had grabbed a revolver from somewhere under the bar. Charlie now turned his attention to him. 'Put that revolver on the bar, Len, where I can see it.'

Everyone's attention focused on the revolver which Len reluctantly placed on the bar. It did not escape Charlie's notice, however, that Len surreptitiously moved it towards McGee who was now within arm's length of reaching the gun.

'Do you fancy going for it, McGee?' taunted Charlie. 'Go on, go for it.'

'He'd never stand a chance,' pointed out one of the onlookers. 'You'd gun him down before he could touch the gun.'

'If he's as fast as he's supposed to be, he can reach it before I fire. I'm holding my gun down by my side. That gives him a chance, doesn't it?'

McGee considered the options. There was no doubt that he was in danger of being shot. Charlie Sankey wouldn't just walk away from the confrontation. It would mean that he would lose face to such an extent that he wouldn't be able to face the Circle T cowboys in the future. He would be a figure of scorn, and cowboys, while for the most part were an easy-going bunch of men, once they spotted one among them who had a weakness could be cruel in the extreme with their innuendoes and taunts. McGee knew that there was only one choice for him.

To Charlie's surprise McGee, instead of inching towards the revolver, moved a foot or so away from the bar.

'What's the matter, McGee, are you yellow?' sneered Charlie.

McGee's answer took him completely by surprise. Before he could raise his gun, McGee had vaulted over the bar. Charlie fired at the airborne figure but the shot went over McGee's head. McGee had grabbed the revolver with his other hand as he leaped over the bar. He fired one shot. It sent Charlie's gun spinning out of his hand.

Charlie let out a bloodcurdling scream. 'You bastard, you've broken my hand.'

'That's nothing to what you were going to do to me, remember?' He watched dispassionately as the blood dripped from Charlie's right hand. Several of the onlookers, surmising correctly that the altercation was over, stepped forward to stem the flow of blood from Charlie's hand. Len, the barman, handed them a towel.

At that moment the sheriff and his deputy stepped into the bar.

'I see there's been a disagreement,' said the sheriff drily, glancing at Charlie's bloodied hand.

'He pulled a gun on me,' announced McGee. 'If you'd got here earlier you could probably have saved Charlie's hand.'

'I assume that you are the one who shot him,' said the sheriff.

'That's right, it was the smartest piece of shooting I've seen in all the years I've been in this bar,' enthused Len. 'McGee vaulted over the bar before Charlie could get in a shot. When he did fire it was too late.'

'So you're McGee.' The sheriff was studying McGee's face as though trying to memorize it.

'That's right.' McGee was downing the pint of beer which Len, who was pleased with the outcome of the fight since nobody had been seriously injured, had thoughtfully poured for him.

'We've heard about you,' said the deputy sheriff, who was also eyeing McGee suspiciously.

'That's not surprising. I've been working at the Lazy Y ranch. I work for Mr Taunton. I've been working there for over a year.'

'It's not you as a cowboy we're interested in,'

stated the sheriff. 'It's more your other activities.'

'What other activities?' McGee drained his glass and put it on the bar.

'Let me put it this way – this is the second time you've caused trouble this week.'

'If you're referring to the time when you allowed the locals to have their bit of fun by almost drowning an Indian girl, yes, I did step in to stop somebody getting hurt. I was doing your job for you.'

McGee realized that he had said the wrong thing by the way the sheriff's mouth tightened. The deputy, too, recognized the warning sign.

'McGee brought the guns in that belonged to the person who had started the trouble,' he confirmed.

The sheriff ignored him. He was still staring at McGee. 'I find it strange that there have been two incidents in this peaceful town involving guns and you were in the middle of both.'

'I was an innocent bystander,' protested McGee.

'I've also heard reports that you've been involved in dozens of card-schools this week. And guess who's come up smelling of roses every time.'

'I've played a lot of cards,' confessed McGee.

'Where did you live before you came to Stoneville?'

'New York.'

'So you were a professional gambler before you came here.'

'I was never a professional card-player. I worked in a circus.' McGee was beginning to get annoyed with the questioning. 'Now if you'll excuse me, I've got some business to attend to.' He started to move towards the door.

To his surprise the sheriff barred his way. 'Not so fast, McGee. The only place you'll be going to for the next few days is to jail.'

'You're putting me in jail?' Incredulity stretched McGee's voice.

'You've got it. I'm putting you in jail since you're a public nuisance. Trouble seems to follow you around. The last thing I want in this town is more trouble.'

'But you can't hold me. There's no charge against me.' McGee was half-shouting.

'I don't have to find a charge. There's a state of emergency in the town due to the drought. I've got complete freedom from the county court to take whatever action I think is necessary.'

McGee had visions of the whole scheme to con the townsfolk of some of their money when he would be in a position to announce that the rain was shortly due, all coming to nothing if he was in jail. And all because of this officious sheriff who was standing in front of him. His only alternative was to eat humble pie.

'I swear I won't be any more trouble.' He showed his hands in a familiar gesture of innocence.

The sheriff studied him as though trying to read his mind. After what seemed an eternity McGee detected a softening of the sheriff's face. McGee was an expert in studying men's faces, which was largely why he had been so successful at poker.

'All right, I won't send you to jail.' McGee allowed himself a faint sigh of relief.

McGee's reaction was short lived. 'Instead I'm sending you back to the ranch where you work. The deputy will go with you. You will not be allowed to put a foot inside the town until I say so.'

McGee shook his head in disbelief. 'You can't do that.'

'Oh, yes, I can.'

'Oh, yes, he can,' echoed the deputy.

As the deputy led McGee out of the saloon there was a cheer from some of the watchers. McGee reflected gloomily that whereas half an hour before he had been the hero, he was now the villain. As if to confirm that his troubles weren't over he looked up at the mountaintop in the distance. There was no doubt about it. There was the distinct evidence of smoke – the sort of signs that would be apparent if Tandolee was sending him a smoke signal saying that rain was imminent.

CHAPTER 8

The smoke that McGee had spotted on top of the mountain was indeed coming from the fire that Salmon and Tandolee had built. Salmon was watching Tandolee regularly cover and uncover the fire to create the smoke signal.

'I see you've done this before,' said Salmon.

She flashed him a smile. 'My grandfather once showed me how they used to send messages by using smoke signals. He showed me how we used to call other tribes together in order to start a battle. Do you want me to show you?'

'No,' cried Salmon, with alarm. 'The last thing we want is to start another Indian war.'

'I don't think there's any danger of that,' she replied bitterly. 'They've all been herded on to the reservation like cattle.'

'I'm sorry,' said Salmon, inadequately. 'I know life hasn't been easy for you.'

'Yes, it was a struggle.' She was still raising and lowering the blanket over the fire. 'Then you saved my life and changed everything.'

'I've been meaning to talk about that.'

'About what?' She regarded him with luminous eyes.

He was plainly embarrassed. 'This business of you being my squaw. It isn't serious, is it?'

'Of course it is.' She flared up angrily. In fact her anger caused her to stop creating smoke from the fire. 'It is one of our unwritten laws. It is just as binding as your law which says an eye for a tooth.'

Salmon smiled.

'I don't see what's funny.'

'It's an eye for an eye.'

'Well whatever.'

'As I've already explained to you before, I'm already married. And according to our laws we can only have one wife.'

'I'm not another wife. We haven't slept together – although I've given you several chances while we've been up here on the mountain.'

Salmon recollected the occasions – all at night, when she had crept under his blanket. He knew that one move from him and Tandolee would be in his arms. She was a beautiful Indian and any man would be happy for her to become his lover. But not for him. He was devoted to his darling Jill and not even the temptation of Tandolee curling up under his blanket could make him forget his marriage vows.

Salmon tried another tack. 'Haven't you a boyfriend? An attractive young lady like yourself must have one.'

'Well there's Summer Lightning, he's – what you would call my boyfriend.'

'Where is he now?'

She had resumed the methodical rising and lowering of the blanket. 'He's on the reservation.'

'Does he love you?'

'We do not talk about love the way you and your people do.'

'I don't understand.'

'The fact that we don't talk about it doesn't mean we don't love. If you had slept with me I would have loved you until my dying day. If necessary I would die for you.'

Salmon turned away to hide his embarassment.

There followed a long silence where each was busy with their own thoughts. At last Tandolee said: 'How much longer do I have to keep doing this?'

'1 think you can stop now. McGee must have noticed it. '

'What do we do next?'

'We go back down to the town.'

Tandolee climbed on to a rock. She stared out westwards. 'The clouds don't seem to be moving much,' she announced.

'That's a good thing,' stated Salmon. 'It will give McGee more time to collect the money.'

They began to pack up their blankets. When they had each rolled up their few possessions, Salmon coughed.

Tandolee glanced up at him. 'What is it?'

'I'd – I'd just like to say that I've enjoyed your company enormously.'

They were standing close together and after a while she nodded slowly. 'I feel the same.'

They stayed staring at each other for several moments. Then Salmon said: 'I think it's time for us to go.'

They started on their way down the mountain. Their camp on the top of the mountain was a couple of thousand feet high but they were following a narrow path and the descent was easy.

'There's one thing I would like to do before we get to the town,' said Tandolee.

'What's that?'

'I'm stinking of smoke after making those signals. The river starts flowing just below us.' She pointed to the place where he could see a pool of water which announced the start of the river. 'I'm going to have a wash.'

'Go ahead.'

Salmon sat on the bank and began to roll a cigarette. His attention was fixed on his activity and it wasn't until he looked up, having succeeded in lighting the cigarette, that he had a shock. Tandolee had completely divested herself of her clothes. She was standing naked by the edge of the pool. She stood there for a few seconds as though challenging him to look away. She made a perfect picture as though posing for one of those newfangled cameras. Salmon knew that the moment was one he would always carry with him in his mind. Eventually, with a smile, she dived into the pool.

CHAPTER 9

In the nearest large town of Herford, the drought in Stoneville was a regular topic of conversation. One particular group who were discussing it consisted of five men who were known collectively as the Finley gang. Individually they were known as Miller, Stolley, Gimlet, Bling and their leader, Lance Finley. They were the most wanted outlaws in the territory.

The reason they had come to Herford several weeks before was because they thought there would be easy pickings by robbing one of the several banks in the town. However they had soon discovered that security in the banks was at a premium and there would be considerable risk involved in trying to rob one of them. So they had settled into an easy existence of spending most of the time in one or other of the town's saloons.

'Why is it that they are suffering from a drought in Stoneville and we've plenty of water here?' demanded Bling.

If intelligence tests had been invented at the time he would have scored considerably lower marks than his companions.

'It's obvious. Because Stoneville is twenty-five miles away,' said Stolley.

He was the oldest of the group and considered himself more intelligent than the others – with the exception perhaps of Finley.

'Twenty-five miles isn't far,' said Bling. 'We could ride there in a day.'

'One of the reasons why we aren't suffering from the drought is that we get our rain from the north. From Canada in fact.' The statement was supplied by Miller.

'From Canada.' Bling considered the prospect with incredulity.

'That's right,' supplied Stolley. 'If you look at the direction of the river flowing though the town you'll see that it flows from the north. It brings the town's water from Canada.'

'But Canada's miles away, and it's another country.'

'Listen, you silly fool, it doesn't matter what

country it's in. If the river flows from there then it brings water to the town.' Stolley was beginning to lose his temper.

'All right, that's enough.' Finley held up his hand showing that the argument shouldn't develop any further. 'I think that Bling has made an important point.'

'I have?' Bling's answer managed to convey both surprise and pleasure. It wasn't often that he was praised by their leader. In fact the opposite was more often the case. If there were any insults to be hurled about then he would invariably be the recipient.

'How has he said anything clever?' said Gimlet. He was the fastest gun of the group and his lightning speed in drawing and firing his revolver had helped them get out of trouble on several occasions.

'Yes, what did he say?' Miller, too, who was generally considered to be a man of few words was drawn into the discussion.

'He said it was only twenty-five miles to Stoneville.'

'I know. But everybody knows that.' A slightly deflated Bling was forced to accept the fact that what had somehow been considered to be an intelligent remark by their leader was in fact a common, mundane one.

'Which we could cover in a day,' continued Finley, remorselessly.

Stolley spotted in which way the conversation was leading. 'So you think we should go there?'

Finley favoured him with a smile of approval, like a teacher whose favourite pupil had just grasped a mathematical theorem.

'Exactly.'

'But they haven't got any water there,' stated Stolley.

'That will suit you. You won't have to wash so often,' said Bling.

Stolley showed signs of rising to the bait. 'Listen you—' he began threateningly.

Finley again raised his hand to rule an end to the bickering.

'I don't know anything about Stoneville, but I would guess it's a hick town with, say, three banks at the most. They should be a sitting target for us, since the locals will have been so busy trying to cope with the drought that they'll hardly have time to bother with any outlaws who want to relieve their bank of its money.'

The other four digested the statement in silence.

Eventually Miller said: 'I think it's a good idea.'

There was a murmur of agreement. The loudest 'yes' came from Bling. After all, it had been due to his having mentioned how far it was to Stoneville that Finley had thought of the idea.

'We'll start at sun-up tomorrow,' stated Finley. 'We'll have to get extra water-carriers from the store. And take extra rations with you. We don't want to have to go into the town to buy food.'

'And you'd better have a bath before you go.' Bling couldn't resist having a last snipe at Stolley, who aimed a kick at him.

'All right, that's enough,' said Finley, sharply. 'We've got to get some provisions. So let's move.' He suited his action to the statement by rising from his chair.

'Stoneville, here we come,' said Bling.

The others favoured him with a smile, with the exception of Stolley.

CHAPTER 10

Every step that his horse took away from Stoneville drove a dagger ever deeper into McGee's heart. They were riding away from the best source of easy money he had ever been involved in – and he had been involved in a few, particularly when they had lived in New York. And all because of that officious sheriff.

McGee glanced across at the deputy, who was riding by his side. Perhaps an appeal to his better nature might resolve the unbearable situation.

'Can't you let me go back into town? I promise I'll keep out of trouble.'

'You can say that again. You'll be out of trouble because you'll be staying at the ranch.'

McGee gave it one more try. 'My friend will be looking for me in the town. He won't know where I am.'

'Is he the big guy who pulled the Indian out of the river.'

'Yes, that's him.'

'If I see him I'll tell him where you are.'

'Thanks for nothing.'

'Don't mention it.'

Further conversation dried up. It was only when they had covered a couple more miles that the deputy came up with an opening gambit.

'Why do you keep looking up at the mountain?'

'I'm looking at the smoke signal.'

'What smoke signal?' The deputy followed the direction McGee had kept glancing at. 'Oh, yes, I see it. Are you sure it's a smoke signal?'

'Of course I am.' If the deputy had only known it McGee was speaking with one hundred per cent certainty.

'I've never seen any of those before.' The deputy was fascinated by the plumes of smoke which rose at regular intervals.

'You haven't been around much, have you.'

The deputy ignored the gibe. 'So who do you think caused them?'

'I don't think. I know. It's an Indian.'

'We don't get many Indians in Stoneville. Except that Indian girl.' They had drawn up their horses and the deputy was still staring at the smoke signal. 'What do you think is behind it?'

McGee wondered what the deputy would say if he told him the truth. Regretfully he dismissed the idea. 'Perhaps it's the beginning of an Indian uprising.'

The deputy swung round in his saddle in order to decide whether McGee was joking. But McGee had put on his poker-face and there was no tell-tale sign whether he was telling the truth or not.

'They can't be. We'd have had a telegram from the sheriff in Herford if there was any danger of the Indians starting any trouble.'

McGee decided to rub salt into the wound. 'I've been around quite a bit. Those signals look rather ominous to me.'

The deputy was still studying them. 'Yes, they do seem to have been going on for a long time.' For the first time uncertainty had crept into his voice.

'Perhaps we'd better turn back so that you can warn the sheriff that there could be trouble from the Indians.'

It was a long shot but when you don't have any good cards in your hand, McGee decided that it was worth playing.

The deputy dashed any hopes that McGee

might be harbouring with his next remark. 'I've got a better idea. You go on ahead to the ranch, you know the way, at least your horse does. I'll go back to tell the sheriff about the smoke signals. He'll know how to deal with them. He's a lot older than I am. He fought in the Indian wars. You don't need a nursmaid from here on.'

'Huh! Some nursemaid,' retorted McGee, as the deputy turned and started galloping back to Stoneville.

In Herford a rather unusual conversation was taking place involving three characters whom McGee had met on a previous visit to the town. The three were Dan Jackson, his daughter, Daisy, and their Indian helper. Harold.

'You're going to do what?' Daisy, who was a pretty young woman, addressed the remark to her father.

'I'm going to stop selling whiskey,' her father replied, calmly. 'At least for the present.'

Dan's whiskey was as much a part of Herford as any of the town's buildings. He had been brewing it and selling it in the town's weekly market for several years. At first it had been met with considerable hostility by the churchgoing members of the public. But eventually they had accepted the inevitable situation and concluded that if Dan didn't sell his whiskey in the market then some outsider would move in and take over. Truth to tell many of the churchgoers themselves would buy a bottle to sustain them throughout the week. 'It's only for medicinal purposes,' they would inform their wives. A statement which had been repeated by Dan on dozens of occasions.

'You're giving up selling whiskey?' Harold, who was normally a man of few words, joined in the discussion.

'It's only temporary,' Dan explained. 'I'm going to sell water instead.'

'Water.' Daisy began to laugh. She laughed so much that tears began to roll down her cheeks. Even Harold, whose facial expressions were as limited as his conversation, permitted himself a smile.

'You've been out too much in the sun,' Daisy announced eventually. 'Either that or you've been drinking too much of your whiskey.'

For answer Dan produced a newspaper with a flourish. 'See this.' He pointed to the headline.

They were seated in their caravan and Daisy moved across to see what had caused her father's outburst.

The headline of the local paper stated: DROUGHT REACHES ITS THIRD MONTH IN

STONEVILLE. There followed a description of the privation of the inhabitants of the town including how many of the cattle were being prematurely destroyed because they couldn't be fed. When Daisy had finished the article she glanced up at her father.

'So you think we should go to Stoneville to sell them water?'

'For a girl who inherited your mother's beauty it seems that you also share some of my brains,' said Dan.

'I'm not a girl, I'm a woman,' said Daisy angrily.

Dan waved a dismissive hand. 'Well whatever.'

'Assuming we go to Stoneville to sell water, what's going to happen to the business here? What about the still and all the equipment?'

'I've thought of that. Bernard can look after things.'

'Bernard?'

'Yes, he's sweet on you. He'd be even sweeter if you'd give him a little more encouragement.'

'Bernard is a nice boy. He's got a lot of good points.'

'But you don't love him?'

Daisy shrugged her shoulders.

'Don't say you're still pining for that married man – what was his name?'

'McGee? It was months ago when he was here. Anyhow I've got over him.'

Her father flashed her a suspicious glance.

'When are we going to go?' she asked.

'As soon as possible. I've got to see Bernard and arrange things with him. You two can start filling the bottles.'

'How much are you going to charge for the water?'

'Two dollars a bottle.'

'Two dollars a bottle?' demanded Daisy, incredulously.

'I could probably get more but I wouldn't want to fleece my fellow man,' her father said, with mock piety.

'Since when?' demanded Daisy. For reply her father flung a cushion at her.

CHAPTER 11

Salmon and Tandolee completed their descent down the mountain. Salmon headed for the spot where he had left his horse. A young boy was lying on the grass. He stood up when Salmon approached.

'I've been looking after your horse, mister,' he announced. 'I gave her water and some oats.'

'Thanks.' Salmon tossed him a coin which he caught adroitly. 'What happened to the other horse that was tied up here?'

'The feller who rode it went off some time ago.'

'Went off? How long ago?'

'I'm not sure. About an hour maybe?'

'Thanks.' Salmon was about to leave when the boy's next words stopped him in his tracks.

'He went off with the deputy sheriff.'

'Are you sure?'

71

'Of course I'm sure. I know the deputy. He's caught me often enough and dragged me off to school.

The remark brought a smile from Tandolee but put a worried frown on Salmon's face.

'Why would he want to go off with the deputy?'

'I heard the deputy say that he was taking him back to the ranch.'

Salmon groaned. 'Something's gone wrong.'

'You don't know that for sure,' said Tandolee. 'Maybe the boy didn't hear the message correctly.'

'There's nothing wrong with my hearing,' said the boy, sullenly.

'There's only one way to find out what happened,' said Salmon. 'I'll have to go into one of the saloons. Someone there would be bound to know.'

In fact the information was easily obtained from the first saloon Salmon entered. Len, the barman of the Wind and Whistle revealed it with obvious delight.

'McGee was in a gunfight with Charlie, who was one of the regulars.'

'But McGee wasn't carrying a gun,' protested Salmon.

'I know. But the way he won the fight was one

of the smartest moves I've seen in all the years I've been a barman. He vaulted over the bar and before Charlie could get a clear shot at him, he'd shot Charlie's hand.'

'McGee was an acrobat in a circus,' supplied Salmon. 'But what happened after the gunfight?'

'The sheriff arrived. He said that McGee had been involved in a previous fight. That he was a troublemaker and so he should go back to the ranch. The deputy went with him.'

Salmon informed Tandolee, who since she was an Indian, hadn't been allowed in the saloon, about the gunfight and McGee's forced exit from the town.

'What are we going to do now?' She gazed at him with her luminous eyes.

'I'm not sure.' They were walking down Main Street.

'Have you got any money?'

'Only a few dollars. McGee would have had some money. He would have won it by playing poker.'

'How far is the ranch where you work?'

'About seven miles. It's an hour's ride.'

'We'll have to go there and get the money from McGee.'

They hurried to the spot where Salmon had

left his horse. There was no sign of the boy who had been there before. So much for him looking after the horse, thought Salmon, as he untied the mare.

Salmon swung into the saddle and Tandolee jumped up behind.

'Are you sure you're all right?' demanded Salmon.

'You forget I'm an Indian. I was riding a horse before I was a year old,' came the answer.

When they eventually approached the ranch there was very little activity. Usually there would be a dozen or more cowboys hanging around the bunkhouse, having completed their roping and branding for the day. In fact the only person in sight was McGee who had been watching their progress from the coral. He waved a greeting as they approached.

'You found me, then?' He watched as they dismounted from Salmon's horse.

'I hear you managed to get into some more trouble,' said Salmon.

'Never mind about that now. I've got thirty dollars. Is the rain due?' he directed the question at Tandolee.

'It should be here some time tomorrow. It's difficult to say exactly when.'

'Good. If you two ride back to Stoneville you

can start challenging some of the locals to bet you. Tell them that the rain will come in tomorrow. You should be able to get excellent odds on such a bet – at least ten to one.'

'Hang on,' said Salmon. 'We've just got here. The least we'll want is a cup of coffee before we go back. Oh, and I'll take your horse. My horse has galloped most of the way here.'

'Oh, all right, if you must waste time,' said McGee ungraciously.

About half an hour later the two set off back to Stoneville, this time on McGee's horse. The sun was still high in the sky. There was no sign of any clouds as Salmon's regular gaze at the sky confirmed.

This time Salmon left the horse in the livery stable. He tossed the owner a dollar.

'I'm afraid there isn't much water,' he was informed. 'I've got to ration it out.'

Salmon and Tandolee started walking down Main Street.

'Are you going into the saloons as McGee suggested?' she asked.

'I don't see what else I can do. That's where he won the money by playing at cards.'

'Yes, but you don't know who the gamblers are. And maybe McGee took their money from them. In which case they wouldn't be able to place a bet on the rain coming.'

'What do you suggest?'

'That we do what my father and I used to do. We get a soap box to stand on. It will attract a crowd. Then we get them to place their bets.'

'Yes, that sounds a quicker way of doing it,' said Salmon, thoughtfully.

'There's a general store,' said Tandolee. 'I guess he'll let me have a box.'

Her guess was right as five minutes later she returned proudly carrying a small crate.

'That doesn't look strong enough to hold me,' protested Salmon.

'It's not supposed to hold you. I'm the one who'll be doing the talking. I've done it before.'

Tandolee chose a site at the end of Main Street. She stood on the box.

'All right, gather round,' she shouted. 'I'm the person you tried to drown a week ago, but I'm not here to get my revenge. That incident was about an argument over the rain. Some of you blamed me for starting the drought. But that's all nonsense. I can no more start a drought than I can stop the moon from shining. But one thing I can do – I can tell you when this drought is going to come to an end. Some of you know that my father was a rainman – he could bring rain. Well, I can tell you when it is going to rain.'

'When is it going to rain?' asked one of the crowd, which by now had grown to a fairly considerable size.

'Some time tomorrow,' Tandolee replied unhesitatingly.

'A likely story,' sneered the interrupter.

'My friend here – who some of you may remember saved me from the river – has faith in my prediction. He is willing to bet anyone here that what I am saying is true.'

Many of the crowd looked up at the sky. It was completely cloudless.

'I'll take on that bet,' said one. 'What odds will you give?'

'Ten to one,' replied Salmon.

'I'll accept that,' said one.'I'll bet five dollars.'

'All right, I'll take five-dollar bets,' said Tandolee.

There was a general chorus of approval. Salmon nodded to Tandolee.

'How do we know you can cover the bets?' asked another member of the crowd.

Salmon produced the bundle of notes which McGee had been busy collecting from losing card-players during the week. He flicked through them quickly so that the onlookers couldn't see what denomination they were. His sleight of hand was obviously sufficient to impress the onlookers.

'Let's get this straight,' said the principal spokesman. 'You'll bet us that it will rain in the next twenty-four hours – before two o'clock tomorrow.'

'That's right,' stated Salmon. 'The odds are ten to one. I'll take five-dollar bets because they'll be easier.'

'And it will be easier for you to pay out fifty dollars when you lose,' said a wag. There was general laughter.

Tandolee went around collecting the names of those who were prepared to accept the bet. McGee had thoughtfully supplied her with a book of tickets – of the kind used to guarantee entry to a circus or theatre. She wrote the person's name in an exercise-book before giving him one of the tickets.

'Bring this ticket with you tomorrow to collect your fifty dollars,' she repeated at regular intervals.

At the end of collecting the names Tandolee went up to a caravan which was parked at the edge of the small square.

'Are you going to take up the bet?' she asked the attractive girl, about her own age, who was sitting on the steps.

The reply came in the form of a question.

'Isn't that Salmon, who's helping you with the bet?'

'That's right.'

'I thought it was.'

'Have you met him?'

'Yes, I've met him,' replied Daisy. 'But I'm more familiar with his friend, McGee. Where is he, by the way?'

'He's back in the ranch. He's had some trouble with the sheriff.'

'Yes, that sounds like McGee. I'll take one of the bets.'

'What name shall I put down?' demanded Tandolee.

'Daisy. Just Daisy. McGee will remember me.'

When Tandolee returned to where Salmon was standing she showed him the list of people who had taken up the bet. Salmon was impressed.

'There must be almost fifty names here,' he said, excitedly, as he examined the exercise-book.

'By the way, there's a young lady in that cara-van at the far end of the square who says she knows you.' A certain coldness had crept into Tandolee's voice. 'She says her name is Daisy.'

'Daisy? Oh, yes.' Recognition flooded in.

'She's very pretty.'

'She means nothing to me. She was McGee's girlfriend.'

'But I thought you two were married.'

'Yes, well I'm afraid that for a while McGee forgot that he was a married.'

Tandolee's next remark Salmon chose to ignore. 'It's a pity you couldn't follow his example,' she said, with more than a hint of bitterness in her voice.

CHAPTER 12

Salmon and Tandolee rode more slowly back to the ranch than when they had left it a few hours earlier. McGee was waiting for them with eager anticipation.

'Well, how was it?'

'Tandolee was marvellous. She gave a speech. At the end of it the crowd couldn't wait to place their bets.'

McGee glanced appreciatively at Tandolee.

'It looks as though we would make a good team.'

'Your ex-girlfriend was among the crowd.'

'Who's that?'

'Daisy,' supplied Salmon. 'The one we met when we were in Herford.'

'Oh, yes, Daisy,' said McGee, dismissively. 'Tell me, what odds did you get for the bets?'

'Ten to one,' said Salmon.

'I must have collected about fifty names,' said Tandolee. 'You'll find them all in here.'

Tandolee handed the exercise-book to McGee. He glanced at it briefly.

'Each bet is for ten dollars,' stated Salmon.

'You say fifty names. That would mean – let me see – fifty times five. That would make two hundred and fifty dollars. We'd be rich.' He hugged Tandolee excitedly.

She stepped away from his grasp.

'All we've got to do now is to pray that the rain doesn't arrive after two o'clock tomorrow.'

'That's the deadline?'

'Yes, that was the time we agreed on,' said Salmon.

There were a few cowboys hanging around the corall and they glanced interestedly at the trio.

'What are we going to do about Tandolee?' demanded Salmon.

'I've fixed up with the cook that she can have some chow in the kitchen.'

'What about tonight? Where will she sleep?'

'I'll be all right,' she stated. 'I'll sleep under the stars.'

'There won't be any need to. There's an attic in the house. The housekeeper said you can use that. Unless, of course, you and Salmon prefer to sleep outside.'

Salmon made a playful threatening fist.

'The attic sounds fine,' said Tandolee. 'I'll sleep like a log, as usual. I hope you'll sleep well, McGee. If you don't you can always try counting all that money you'll have when you win the bet.'

In Stoneville Daisy too was discussing the bet.

'I wonder what McGee is up to. There's no way that the Indian girl can foretell whether it's going to rain. It must be some trick or other.' She turned to one of the other two occupants of the caravan. 'Harold, you're a Crow Indian, can you tell when the rain is going to come?'

'I can't even tell the time.'

Dan smiled.

'She must have collected about fifty names. That would mean that McGee would collect say two hundred and fifty dollars if it rains.' She was worrying the situation like a kitten with a ball of wool.

'It doesn't bother me,' said Dan, trying to stretch out his legs in the rather cramped caravan.

'Of course if he loses he'll have to pay out over two thousand dollars. Where will he get that kind of money?'

'Don't worry your pretty head about him,' said Dan. 'All that concerns us is whether we can sell the rest of our stock before it rains.'

'I was very impressed with the speech the Indian girl made,' continued Daisy.

'Her name is Tandolee. Yes, she's a very clever person. She was educated by the missionaries,' stated Harold.

'Why didn't they educate you?' demanded Daisy.

'I never wanted to go to school. Anyhow I'm useful. I'm the best tracker in the territory.'

'I'll give you that,' said Dan. 'Now you can stack the bottles so that we'll be ready to start selling them first thing in the morning.'

At the ranch McGee was the first to rise in the morning. He went to the bunkhouse window. The sun was rising in what appeared to be a clear blue sky.

He gave Salmon a dig in the ribs.

'Get up,' he said. 'You've got a busy day in front of you.'

After breakfast they went to collect Tandolee, who was having her meal in the kitchen.

'Did you sleep well, McGee?' she enquired as she munched a piece of toast.

'Hurry up,' he said, impatiently. 'You and Salmon have to ride into town.'

'What's the hurry?' she enquired. 'The bet isn't due to become paid up until after it rains.'

'I know that. But it's important for you to be

84

seen in town to show that we're not welshing on the bet. Just show your face around the town.'

'All right,' she conceded. 'But there's one condition.'

'What's that?'

'That you let me borrow your horse. There's not much room in the saddle on Salmon's horse for both of us.'

Somewhat reluctantly, McGee agreed.

About half an hour later they set out. Salmon was carrying an extra saddle-bag.

'You'll want that for the money,' said McGee.

'Don't you wish you were coming with us?' demanded Tandolee.

'It would be too risky,' said Salmon, who had taken her words at their face value, not realizing that she was secretly teasing McGee.

'As long as you bring the lovely money back, I'll be happy,' came the reply.

'I'll race you,' said Tandolee.

They galloped towards the town, happily confident that in a few hours' time they would have pulled off a memorable confidence trick.

CHAPTER 13

In a clearing a couple of miles outside Stoneville Finley was screaming abuse at Bling. In fact he was shouting so loudly that it was a good thing they were in a deserted spot, or any interested eavesdropper would have heard the contents of his abuse.

'You idiot! You fool! You half-wit! Don't you know what you've done?'

'I told you I took up the bet about the rain.'

'You told me you took up the bet about the rain.' Finley was not shouting now, nevertheless he managed to emphasize every word. The rest of the outlaws were regarding the one-sided confrontation with interest.

'I put your name down on the list as well,' protested Bling.

'Oh, my God! Why do I have to put up with such a numskull?' Finley appealed to the Almighty in vain.

Initially the others hadn't grasped the reason for Finley's outburst, but now it dawned on them.

'I suppose you put my name down as well,' snapped Stolley.

'Yes.'

'And mine?' demanded Miller.

'Yes.'

By now it occurred to Bling that his impetuous action yesterday wasn't being too well received by the others.

'And mine?' growled Gimlet.

'Yes,' said a by now completely cowed Bling.

'I told you we shouldn't have let him out of our sight,' said Stolley.

'Let me shoot him now and we won't have any more cock-ups like this,' pleaded Gimlet.

Finley ignored the suggestion. 'You wrote our names down in the book?'

'Well no. I didn't write our names down—'

'He can hardly write, anyhow,' interrupted Stolley.

'I gave the Indian girl our names,' he said, feeling that perhaps by putting the record straight all this ill-feeling which he had apparently generated would somehow evaporate.

'And did you go to the sheriff's office and write down in his book that we came here to rob a bank?'

'Of course not.' Bling realized that he had made a mistake in giving their names to the Indian girl, but surely it wasn't as serious a matter as Finley and the others were making out.

'What do you think is going to happen after we've robbed the bank, half-wit?' said Stolley.

'We'll move on to another town, as we usually do.'

'And why have we been so successful up until now in robbing banks?'

'Because we're quite good at it.'

'Because we're quite good at it. And because nobody knows who we are.' This time Stolley was shouting.

At last Bling was beginning to see why he had erred in giving their names to the Indian girl.

'But now every sheriff in the territory will know who we are. When we've robbed the bank the sheriff will go through the list of names. He'll know the people who are living in the town. He'll be looking for five names that he hasn't come across before. And there they'll be. Staring him in the face. Our names. Which you've very kindly given him.'

Now that it had been spelled out to him, Bling realized the enormity of his mistake.

'I didn't think. . . .'

'You didn't think. Well, I suppose you've got to

have a brain to be able to think, and you've never had much to start with,' snapped Stolley.

'Wait a minute, there might be a way out of this,' said Finley. 'The Indian girl won't realize the importance of the fact that our names are on her list. Right?'

'Right,' echoed Bling, who was grasping at a straw that somehow there might be a way out of this mess that he had been responsible for.

'You say that she wrote the names down in a book?'

'Yes, an old exercise-book. The kind we used to have in school.'

'How would you know? You never went to school,' growled Stolley.

'All right, that's enough bickering. We can assume that the Indian hasn't looked at the names. How many were there in the book?'

'She filled up a few pages.' Bling volunteered the information eagerly.

'And when is this bet due?'

'The bet is that it will rain some time before two o'clock today.'

'So some time this morning we've got to get hold of the exercise-book.'

'Yes, I suppose if we could get hold of it, then we would all be in the clear,' agreed Stolley.

'Who was she with? Was she on her own?'

demanded Finley.

'No, there was a big guy with her. He was handing out the tickets so that we can collect our money if we win the bet.'

'Or he takes the money if they win the bet,' supplied Miller, who was known among the outlaws as a betting man.

'We've got to look for these two,' said Finley. 'We've got to get that exercise-book at all costs. Even if it means killing the pair of them to get it.'

CHAPTER 14

Salmon and Tandolee rode into Stoneville and left their horses in the livery stable. They were walking down Main Street when somebody called out a greeting. They turned and saw Miss Brown on the opposite sidewalk. They crossed over to meet her.

'I thought I recognized the dress,' said Miss Brown, with a smile. 'And I couldn't mistake this big figure here.'

'Thank you for the dress,' said Tandolee. 'Although I hope I might be able to afford to buy one for myself soon.'

'Yes, it doesn't really do your figure justice,' said Miss Brown, surveying the dress critically. 'So you two are going shopping, are you?'

'Not until tomorrow,' replied Salmon.

'What happens tomorrow?' demanded a puzzled Miss Brown.

'It's a long story,' said Tandolee.

'I've got a suggestion. Why don't you two come to my house and have a cup of coffee. Then you can tell an inquisitive old spinster all about it.'

Tandolee glanced at Salmon, who nodded his acceptance of the offer.

When they were seated in Miss Brown's parlour and sipping their coffee, Tandolee began her story. She explained how she and her father had tricked people in several towns by pretending that they could foretell when rain was coming. Actually it had depended on her relaying a message by means of a smoke signal from the top of a mountain to her father in the town. He had accepted bets on the probability of rain coming and they had inevitably won the bets. Then her father had died. 'And that was the end of that,' Tandolee concluded.

'But you've got something else up your sleeve for this town?' enquired Miss Brown.

'That's right. We're going to pull the same trick here. We've bet around fifty of the locals that rain will come today – before two o'clock.'

'I'd say you're taking a chance – a big chance. The rain could come later in which case you would lose your bet.'

'The bet has been successful before,' said

Tandolee, with a hint of stubborness in her voice.

'I'm sure you know what you're doing, my dear. And it will be a good thing for you get your own back on the crowd of hooligans who almost drowned you.'

The pair left Miss Brown's house. They instinctively looked up at the sky. There were a few wispy clouds but nothing that signified that it would rain in a few hours' time.

'It doesn't look much like rain,' stated Salmon.

'There's plenty of time yet,' said Tandolee, airily.

'What are we going to do now?' asked Salmon.

'You can go into the saloon and have a drink.'

'What are you going to do?'

'There are a couple of shops here that sell dresses. I'm going to look at some of them. I won't be able to buy them until tomorrow, but I'll know what I'll be going to buy.'

They separated. Tandolee went further along Main Street where the first of the two ladies' clothes shops was situated. The shop announced that it was a draper's shop by having a young lady in the window who was busy at a sewing-machine.

Tandolee spent an interesting half of an hour

or so going through the dresses that were for sale. In the end the shop-owner became rather impatient with Tandolee's frequent requests to try on one dress after another.

'I hope you're thinking of buying one of these dresses, young lady,' she said, sharply.

'Oh, yes,' replied Tandolee. 'But not until tomorrow.'

She left the shop and proceeded along the street to the other ladies' clothing shop. She stopped outside. This one didn't have anyone in the window busy at a sewing-machine. Instead it had several dresses which cost considerably more than those in the previous shop.

Her attention was glued to the window when a stranger appeared by her side. At first she took no notice. After all, it wasn't unusual for two or more people to stare in at the window. In fact the shop, being the biggest in Stoneville, actually boasted two windows. It was when the man uttered the threatening words that Tandolee's blood ran cold.

'Don't make any sudden movements, miss. This is a gun I'm holding under my jacket. It's pointing straight at your heart. If I pull the trigger your death will be instantaneous. Do you understand?'

It took a superhuman effort for her to turn

and face the stranger. She knew she had never seen the man before.

'Wha – what do you want with me?' she demanded.

'Just come with me. Behave naturally and you won't get hurt,' said Stolley.

He gave a signal to another man who was standing on the other side of the street. He came across to join them.

'The young lady said she would be delighted to join us,' Stolley said, with grim humour.

CHAPTER 15

In the sheriff's office the usual small gathering was discussing the situation in Stoneville, but this time with the addition of the deputy sheriff.

'I've asked my deputy here to attend this informal meeting,' explained the sheriff, 'because there is an additional matter we need to discuss.'

The deputy nodded to the other two, who acknowledged his presence with a wave of the hand.

'First,' said the sheriff, 'I think we should discuss the subject that has been the chief topic of our conversation for the past three months – the drought. Has anyone any further observations or comments about it?'

The preacher, Tindall, coughed – a sure indication that he was about to impart some knowledge.

'There's a lady in town – I use the term lady

advisedly – who is taking bets that it will rain today.'

'You mean the young Indian girl that we tried to drown,' said the deputy.

The sheriff frowned. He had had second thoughts about the advisability of asking his deputy to attend the meeting, and this confirmed them. He was a young man who often spoke out of turn, when it should be left to his elders to discuss the matters first.

'The Indian girl was given a ducking partly as a means of entertainment because the townsfolk were becoming restless after the effects of the drought,' corrected the sheriff.

'The idiots claimed she was a witch,' stated the deputy.

'How are we to know that she wasn't?' demanded the preacher.

'Because we're living in the late-nineteenth century and not in the seventeenth,' retorted the deputy.

The preacher was about to continue the argument, but the sheriff shook his head.

'We can argue about that for ever. My deputy, however, would like to raise a point of discussion about Indians – not necessarily the one we ducked.'

'I was riding to one of the ranches yesterday

when I spotted something very unusual,' Briers began. He had the full attention of the others. 'It was smoke signals coming from the top of the mountain.'

'Maybe it was somebody putting out a fire,' suggested the doctor.

'It went on for at least half an hour. Nobody would take that long to put out a fire.'

'I remember seeing smoke signals in the days of the Indian wars,' stated the sheriff. 'They nearly always spelled trouble.'

'I'm too young to remember the Indian wars,' supplied the preacher.

'From which mountain did you see the signals?' enquired the doctor.

'The one to the west.'

'Have you noticed any more Indians in the town?' The sheriff directed the question at the preacher.

'I don't think so. Wait a minute, there is one. I haven't seen him before, but I saw him this morning.'

'How far is the nearest reservation?' asked the deputy.

'About two hundred miles,' voiced the doctor. 'I went there once a few years back. The government wanted me to assess the number of TB cases there.'

'What did you find?' enquired the sheriff.

'There were only a few cases of TB but dozens of starvation. I sent in my report and suggested that more food should be distributed to the reservation as a matter of urgency. But nothing was done about it.'

'Well, we'll have to keep a watch on the number of Indians in the town, in case there is something sinister in the smoke signals,' said the sheriff.

'I wonder whether the Indian girl will win her bets,' said the deputy, thinking aloud.

'What was the bet?' enquired the doctor.

'That it will rain some time today. If it does she will get five dollars from each person who accepted the bet.'

'And if it doesn't rain today?'

'She was giving odds of ten to one. That means she will have to pay each person fifty dollars.'

'That seems like very generous odds,' said the doctor, with a smile.

'When I saw her she had a book and she must have collected about fifty signatures. Most of the people who were standing around took up the bet.'

'Did you take up the bet?' demanded the sheriff, keenly.

'Certainly not. I'm not a betting man. And

anyhow why should I bet when I receive such a generous wage from the town.'

The others smiled. The subject of the small amount that the deputy received in payment had been a constant topic of complaint from him during the couple of years which he had served as deputy.

'Never mind, when I retire soon and you have my position you will receive sufficient recompense for your service to the town,' said the sheriff.

'God will repay,' quoted the preacher.

'Well I wish he'd hurry up. There's a very smart young lady who came in yesterday by caravan. She and her father are selling bottles of water. If I had enough money I'd ask her to come out for a meal. But not on the poor wage that I receive.'

'You should have taken up the Indian girl's bet, then you would have had enough money,' said the doctor. The others smiled appreciatively at the joke.

CHAPTER 16

At the Lazy Y ranch McGee kept glancing up at the sky every few minutes. It was mid-morning and there was no sign of the usual thick clouds that always preceded rain.

'Hey, McGee! Come and have a game of poker,' called out one of the cowboys from the bunkhouse.

McGee had taken up his watching position outside the front of the ranch.

'No thanks,' he shouted back.

'He must be sickening for something,' said one of the card-school. 'I've never known McGee refuse to join a card-game before.'

'Maybe he's thinking how he's going to spend all that money when he wins the bet,' said another of the card-school.

'Or maybe he's worrying about how he's going to pay when he loses the bet,' said another. The remark was greeted with raucous laughter.

In fact the thought had crossed his mind several times during the past few hours. What if they lost the bet? What if they had to pay up over $2,000?

In the beginning everything had seemed so sure. Tandolee had said that she and her father had pulled the trick several times in various towns, and it had always succeeded. But what if this was the one town where it wasn't going to succeed? More than likely Stoneville had had a worse drought than any of the previous towns where Tandolee and her father had visited. This could change the scenario. Whereas in the other towns it might be comparatively easy to forecast when it was going to rain, Stoneville could be a different kettle of fish entirely. McGee grew cold at the thought.

What if they lost the bet? McGee had counted the names in Tandolee's excercise- book. There were fifty-three. For the sake of argument, say fifty. If you multiply that by fifty dollars – that meant they would have to pay out $2,500. And how much money did they possess? About thirty dollars which he had painstakingly won at poker during the last week. No wonder he was forced to glance up at the sky every few minutes.

To try to clear the depressing thoughts from

his mind he drew out the exercise-book from his saddle-bag. There was one name which he had noticed when he first glanced at the names. He went down the list until he reached it. Yes, there it was. Daisy. It must be her. Nearly all the others who had placed their bets were men. And hadn't Tandolee said something about Daisy being his ex-girlfriend? He had been so caught up in the excitement of the numbers of bets she and Salmon had collected that the remark had almost gone over his head. But now it surfaced again.

Daisy. Daisy with the pretty face. Daisy, for whom he had almost been tempted to forget his marriage-vows to his wife, Letitia. Yes, they had had quite a time together when he last visited Herford. And now here she was in Stoneville. She was obviously here with her father to sell his whiskey. He wouldn't have thought there was much demand for whiskey when everybody was so short of water. Wait a minute! Maybe that was why Dan had come to Stoneville. To sell water. Yes, that made sense. He would sell his bottles of water twice over. It would be nice to meet Daisy again. Not only was she pretty, but she had a sharp mind. It was a characteristic that most women lacked.

What was Salmon doing now? He was probably enjoying himself in some saloon or other, while he was stuck out here in the wild. They were all in Stoneville, Salmon, Tandolee, and Daisy – all except him. Why should he have to stay at the ranch, when all the excitement would be in Stoneville tonight. During the next few hours, when the rain came and they had won their bet, he should be in town, not out here. The deputy sheriff had said that he had to stay out of town while the drought lasted. Well, it should soon be over. Then the three of them could celebrate together. Or maybe the four of them – since he was sure that he could persuade Daisy to join the celebration.

The more he thought about the idea the more it appealed to him. As soon as it rained they would have won their bet. The fact that it didn't look like rain now shouldn't put him off. Rainclouds were notoriously deceptive in the West. One minute it was sunny and the next it was raining. It was like that rain that they had out in India. What did they call it – the monsoon.

To hell with this inactivity. He went inside the bunkhouse. He was greeted with the usual enquiry about whether he was going to join in the game of cards.

He told them he wanted to borrow a horse. One of the cowboys said he could take his.

McGee thanked him.

Ten minutes later he was galloping towards Stoneville. Salmon would be surprised to see him. And of course there was always the possibility of meeting up again with the delectable Daisy.

CHAPTER 17

The five outlaws had gathered around Tandolee
and were regarding her with a mixture of interest and hostility.

'Why have you brought me here?' demanded
Tandolee, indignantly.

'We'll ask the questions,' said Finley. 'Where is
the exercise-book you put all the names in
yesterday?'

'I don't understand. What do you want the
book for?'

'As I said, I'll ask the questions.' Finley
snapped out the remark. This time there was no
mistaking the hostility in his tone.

Tandolee's mind worked at top speed. Why
would they want the book? There could only be
one answer. She had already deduced that the
five were outlaws. That was the only possible
reason why they had kidnapped her. If they

wanted the exercise-book it could only be because there was something incriminating in it. Like their names. So if their names were in it one of them must have taken up the bets yesterday. She regarded their faces with new interest. But which one?

'I'm not repeating my questions.' Finley was shouting now. 'I want an answer straight away. Do you understand?' He emphasized the point by punching her in the side of her face.

She saw the blow coming and managed to ride most of it, but even with its diminished force it still stung.

'I don't see why I should tell you where it is.'

It wasn't the answer they had expected. It showed in the surprise on their faces. Once Finley had grasped that she was not going to co-operate he hit her again. This time she anticipated the blow and as soon as his fist touched her she fell backwards – to all intents and purposes as a result of the blow.

'You'd better tell us where the exercise-book is, miss, or you'll be beaten black and blue.'

Suddenly it came to her. She recognized the speaker. He had been the one who had taken up the bet. He had been the one who had supplied her with five names. She had thought it strange at the time. Everybody else had taken up the bet in one name – their own. But he had actually given her the names of the other outlaws. If her predicament hadn't been so precarious, she would have found it amusing.

'And what will happen to me after I've told you where the exercise-book is?' she demanded.

'We'll turn you loose. After a reasonable amount of time has passed.' The person who answered this time was the outlaw who had accosted her outside the dressmaker's shop.

'Do you expect me to believe that?' she snapped. 'When you find the exercise-book it won't be of any value to you. But I've seen your faces, and if I go to the sheriff I'm sure I'll be able to give him fairly accurate descriptions of you all. It will only be a matter of time before the law catches up with you.'

'For an Indian you seem quite clever,' said Stolley, grudgingly.

'I told you she made a good speech when she sold the tickets for the bet,' stated Bling.

'Shut up, you fool,' snapped Finley. 'It was because of that we're in this position.'

'So I assume that you don't intend telling us where the book is under any circumstances,' said Stolley.

'You're quite right.'

'In that case there's only one thing to do.' He

directed the remark at Finley.

'Yes, we'll have to persuade you to tell us. It could take some time, and I'll guarantee that it will be a painful process.'

'You do what you have to do,' replied Tandolee.

'We'll give you one last chance,' said Stolley. 'Tell us where the exercise-book is. We'll collect it. Then we'll be on our way. We'll have to take you with us for some of the way. But when we're far enough from Stoneville we'll let you go free.'

'That's a lot better than being beaten,' said Bling, eagerly.

'Thank you for your concern,' said Tandolee. 'But nothing you can say will persuade me to tell you where the book with your names in it is.'

'We've had enough of this kind of talk,' snapped Finley. 'Miller and Gimlet, you two grab her.'

Tandolee realized there was no point in struggling. They half-dragged, half-carried her over to a pine-tree. Miller produced some twine and they tied her securely to the tree.

'We're giving you one last chance to tell us where we will find the book with our names in it.'

Tandolee didn't reply. Finley took off his belt. It was a thick leather belt which was heavy enough to have a holster and revolver attached.

Tandolee had closed her eyes.

'I've got a belt in my hand,' said Finley. He flicked it to make it crack. 'I'm going to beat you until you tell me where the exercise-book is.'

'You do what you have to do,' replied Tandolee. For answer Finley hit her sharply with the belt. Although the pain was excruciating she managed not to cry out.

CHAPTER 18

McGee rode into Stoneville and stabled the borrowed horse at the livery stable. He recognized his own horse and gave it a friendly pat as he passed it. He automatically glanced up at the sky. There were more clouds around than there had been an hour ago, but they still didn't look threatening enough to bring rain. McGee set out to find Salmon.

He found him in the first saloon he entered. It was called the Longhorn and its claim to fame rested in the fact that it was the saloon in Stoneville that catered for staying guests. As part of the excessive payment which the guests would be required to part with in exchange for their draughty room and lacklustre meals the management had arranged for a singer to divert the customers from time to time during the day.

Such a female singer was now entertaining the clientele.

McGee slipped into an empty seat next to Salmon. The singer was belting out the song, *The Yellow Rose of Texas*. When she had finished Salmon burst into rapturous applause. It was then that he realized that McGee was sitting next to him.

His opening gambit was: 'Aren't you suppose to be at the ranch?'

'I don't see any point in staying there. The bet has only got a couple of hours to go.'

Salmon scratched his chin. 'I suppose it could rain before that. All we'd have to do then is to collect our money.'

'I haven't had a drink of beer for the last couple of days,' said McGee, suggestively.

While Salmon was at the bar fetching the drinks a stranger approached McGee.

'Aren't you McGee?' demanded the stranger.

'That's right,' said McGee, warily.

The last time he had been confronted by a stranger in a saloon had led to unexpected and disastrous consequences.

'You don't know me,' continued the stranger, 'but I remember seeing you in New York. It was the cellar where you used to play cards. I remember on one occasion you lost a thousand dollars

112

on one hand.'

'Why is it that everybody remembers the hands that I lost, but not the ones that I won?' demanded an aggrieved McGee.

'I suppose that's life,' said the man, as he turned away.

Salmon returned with the drinks. 'Who's that?'

'Oh, some guy who remembers me from the time we were in New York. By the way, where is Tandolee?'

'She went to look in some of the clothes-shops. She's already thinking how she can spend her winnings.'

'She's a nice girl,' said McGee, sipping his beer.

'She's not a girl, she's a woman,' said Salmon, with annoyance.

'All right. I'm not arguing. You're the one who spent a week with her on the mountain. You should know.'

'There was nothing like that,' snapped Salmon.

'But there could have been?' McGee was fishing for the truth about Salmon's relationship with Tandolee. Not that he believed that Salmon was capable of deceiving his beloved wife, Jill. But you never knew. Still waters ran deep. And

Salmon was the original strong, silent type.

'I've told you I didn't make love to her.' The remark came out stronger than Salmon had intended. A couple of men nearby caught the remark and glanced at Salmon with interest.

'All right, I'll believe you,' said a resigned McGee.

'I think she's had plenty of time to look at the shops now. I think I'll go and find her.'

'I haven't finished my drink,' protested McGee.

'You stay here and finish it. When I find her, I'll bring her back. She'll have to wait outside, since they don't allow Indians inside the saloons.'

Salmon went to search for Tandolee.

The singer had started another song. It was the ever popular *Dixie*. From time to time McGee kept glancing out through the window. The sky was now definitely cloudy. Would the clouds bring rain in time to save their bet?

McGee glanced at his watch. There was less than an hour to go before the bet's deadline. What if they lost? He pushed the thought out of his mind.

The singer finished her song to rapturous applause. McGee went up to the bar to order another drink. The singer, who was standing next to him, said: 'Hullo, handsome, aren't you going to buy me a drink?'

McGee glanced at her. It was difficult to guess her age from the layer of greasepaint on her face and the fact that she was wearing a wig, but he guessed she was older than he had first thought.

'Give the lady a drink,' he told the barman.

'Thanks,' she replied. 'You're a gentleman. Would you like to choose my next song?'

McGee hesitated. He glanced at the door to see whether there was any sign of a returning Salmon. There was none.

'Do you know *Clementine?*'

'Do I know *Clementine?* I was singing it ever since I was twelve. And that was a few years ago, I tell you.'

McGee smiled. He returned to his seat. The pianist struck up the opening bars. The singer didn't go into her song immediately. Instead she said: 'This is for the gentleman in the corner seat.' McGee suddenly found himself the unexpected centre of attention. He gave the singer an acknowledging wave. Why doesn't she get on with it? he whispered to himself through gritted teeth.

She started the song. McGee looked at his watch. Less than half an hour to go and the bet would be lost. A glance through the window confirmed that there did seem to be more dark clouds in the sky.

McGee was on pins to go outside and check whether the darker clouds meant that rain was imminent. He was forced to wait until the singer had finished her song. To his immense annoyance she even gave the chorus a second airing.

When she had finished he was out of his seat like a greyhound out of a trap. He shot out through the door. A quick glance at the sky confirmed what he had already guessed – that the sky was now covered with dark clouds that threatened rain. The snag was that there was no immediate sign of the rain.

'Ten minutes to go, McGee,' the owner of the voice was one of a small group of men who had gathered in the square. They had obviously been some of those who had placed their bets the day before.

'I hope you can cover the bets,' said another. 'I intend buying a horse for my son with my winnings.'

'It will be a change for you to lose,' stated another. 'Every time I've played you at cards, you've won.'

Where was Salmon? And where was Tandolee? At least if they were here he'd have some moral support. And he could do with it the way the crowd was increasing in size.

At last he saw Salmon. He was emerging from the caravan in the distance. McGee had recognized it as belonging to Dan who made the whiskey in Herford.

Salmon spotted McGee and hurried over to him.

'Do you know what time it is?' cried McGee. 'We've only got two minutes to go before we lose our bet.'

'Never mind about the bet,' said a worried Salmon. 'Tandolee has been kidapped. I've searched everywhere for her. In the end I finally went to see whether Dan or his daughter had seen her. It was the Indian who told me what had happened to her. She had been looking in one of the shop-windows when a man came up to her. He was joined by another man. The Indian thinks they forced her to go with them. He thinks the first man was holding a gun under his coat.'

'Why should anyone want to kidnap Tandolee?'

'I don't know. You're the brains of the outfit. You work it out'

At the moment the crowd shouted. 'It's gone two o'clock, McGee, you've lost your bet.'

McGee looked around at the expectant faces in the crowd.

'It never rains, but it pours.' He addressed the remark to Salmon.

'How do you work that out?' demanded Salmon. 'It hasn't started raining yet.'

'It's just a figure of speech,' replied McGee.

CHAPTER 19

'She's passed out,' said Miller.

From the way Tandolee's head was hanging at an unnatural angle the comment seemed a reasonable one.

'You shouldn't have beaten her so much,' Bling voiced his objection to the beating she had been subjected to.

'It was the only way we could get her to tell us where the exercise-book is,' snapped Finley.

'She wasn't going to tell us,' said Gimlet, scornfully. 'She's an Indian. They can take all sorts of punishment without cracking. It's in their make-up.'

'What do we do now?' demanded Miller. 'The time's getting on. The bet will soon be due for payment.'

'That's it,' said Finley, excitedly. 'The bet will be due for payment.'

'I don't see what there is to get excited about,' said Stolley. 'Once the bet is due for payment somebody will consult the book. They'll see five strange names there. They'll put two and two together and it will make five. The five of us.'

Tandolee opened her eyes. 'Water,' she croaked.

Finley nodded to Bling who carried a water-bottle over to her. In his eagerness to give her some water to drink he spilled some down her face. She managed a smile of thanks.

'You might as well untie her,' said Finley. 'She's not going to be any good to us. We'll find another way of getting the incriminating book.'

Bling cut the cord round Tandolee's wrists. She staggered and would have fallen on the ground if Bling had not caught her. She eventually managed to lie on her side so that the red weals didn't touch the ground.

'What time is the bet due?' demanded Finley.

'Two o'clock,' replied Bling.

Finley looked at his watch. 'That's in less than an hour's time. I think we've been wrong in assuming that she had the book She collected the names – yes. But she would have given the book to the feller who was with her.'

'The big feller,' voiced Bling.

'Exactly. Now nobody in the town has seen any of us – except this idiot here.' The others gazed appraisingly at Bling. He hung his head as if to try to escape from their combined gaze.

'So all we have to do is to go into town. Kill the big guy, grab the book in the confusion and then get the hell away from this place.'

'No!' there was a cry of despair from Tandolee.

'Ah! She's got a tongue!' purred Finley.

'Salmon hasn't got the book,' she cried.

'So that's his name – Salmon. Keep talking, young lady. You've given us more information in the past minute than in the previous hour.'

'I wouldn't put any faith in what she says,' stated Stolley. 'It's obvious the two of them were in this together. It's just as obvious that Salmon has got the book. The way she tried to deny it gave her away.'

Even with the excruciating pain Tandolee was able to think clearly. She couldn't put her soul mate, Salmon, in a situation where he would be shot. It would be too unbearable to contemplate.

'I'll tell you where the book is,' she stated.

'Ah! We get there in the end,' said a triumphant Finley.

'First I want a drink of water. Then I want some salt.'

'Why do you want salt?' demanded a puzzled Bling.

'To rub in the weals on her back, of course,' snapped Stolley. 'To stop them getting septic.'

'Get the salt from the saddle-bag,' commanded Finley.

Bling went over to where the horses were tethered. He returned with a bag of salt.

'Who's going to put the salt on her back?' demanded Bling.

'I'll give you one guess.' Finley's eyes were firmly fixed on him.

'Oh, no! Not me.' Bling backed away.

'Please.' Tandolee's eyes implored him.

'But it's going to hurt like hell.'

'No more than the beating I had.'

'Get on with it,' snapped Finley. 'The bet will be over in half an hour. The people who've won will be in the town square expecting to get their money.'

Bling approached the stretched out figure on the grass.

'You'll have to turn over on your front,' he advised. She slowly complied.

Tandolee's dress on her back had been torn to shreds with the repeated blows of the belt. Bling gritted his teeth.

'I'll have to cut some of the rest of the dress

away,' he stated.

'Do what you must,' said Tandolee.

Bling clumsily cut some of the remnants of the dress away in order to expose her back. Miller and Gimlet turned away in revulsion at the sight of the gory weals which criss-crossed her back.

'Get on with it,' half-shouted Finley.

Although the pain was almost unbearable, Tandolee managed to refrain from crying out.

'There, that's finished.' Bling eventually stood back to survey his handiwork.

There was even a note of pride in his voice. 'It's bound to hurt for a few hours.'

'Who do you think you are – some sort of doctor?' snapped Finley.

'So where is the book?' demanded Stolley.

'McGee has got it. He's at the Lazy Y ranch.'

'Who's McGee?'

'He's Salmon's partner.'

'Then why isn't he in town to help to collect the bet?'

'The sheriff told him to stay out of town until the bet was finished.'

'Why would the sheriff do that?'

'Because McGee is a sharpshooter. So is Salmon. They used to be an act in a circus in New York.' There was a hint of pride in her voice when she mentioned Salmon's name.

'I remember something about McGee,' said Bling, eager to impart any scrap of information, on the assumption that by doing so it would help him to return to favour among the outlaws.

'What about him?' demanded Finley.

'When I was in town they said how he had been in a gunfight in a saloon. He had shot the other feller's hand.'

'That's a risky thing to do,' said Gimlet. 'Always go for the head.'

'This isn't getting us anywhere,' snapped Finley.

'If those two are partners it will mean we will be taking on two expert gunslingers,' stated Miller. 'I wouldn't fancy our chances against them.'

Tandolee interrupted the discussion. 'What time is it?'

Stolley consulted his watch. 'Ten minutes past two.'

'We've lost the bet,' said Tandolee, calmly.

'I would think that's the least of your worries,' said Finley, grimly.

CHAPTER 20

McGee faced the crowd who had gathered in the square.

'I've got some good news and some bad news,' began McGee. 'The good news is that those among you who have taken up the bets have won.' He paused.

'What's the bad news?' enquired one of the crowd. 'That you can't pay us?'

'The bad news is that we don't know who have won the bets.'

'But we've got the tickets that your associate gave us.' He held his ticket up to confirm the fact.

'We can't pay out the bets just on the tickets,' said McGee. 'They're tickets you could have kept at home. You could have kept them when you went to see some sort of entertainment, such as a fight, or even a play.'

'Are you saying you can't pay us, then?' There was a distinct note of belligerence in the speaker's voice.

'No, what I'm saying is that I can't pay you until I have the exercise-book with your names in it.'

'So where is the book?'

'If you remember the Indian girl wrote your names in the book. Well she has disappeared. We think she's been kidnapped.'

'Why should anyone want to kidnap her?' demanded one.

'It's a trick to get out of paying us,' stated another.

'That's not true. We want to find the Indian girl. You all saw her when she took your bets yesterday. We think she's been kidnapped and the people who are holding her aren't too far away from the town.'

'What are you going to do about it?' demanded a man from the back of the crowd. 'I can't see the sheriff going to look for her.'

'I wouldn't expect him to. That's where you lot come in. If you form into small search-parties one of the groups is sure to find her. When you do so you will get your money.'

There was some discussion among the crowd. Then one, who was the self-styled spokesman said: 'All right, we'll try to find her. But when we do, we'll want our money.'

'I give you my word,' said McGee.

'That's not worth much,' Daisy informed him, having materialized by his side.

McGee watched the crowd split up into half a dozen groups. Then he turned his attention to Daisy.

'It's lovely to see you again, Daisy.' He attempted to kiss her, but she evaded his arms.

'I don't think it's so lovely to see you. Especially after the way you led me on the last time that we met.'

Salmon, who was feeling rather aggrieved that he had been left out of McGee's plan, said: 'Why don't we go with one of the groups?'

'Because they live in the town. They're more likely to know where to find Tandolee.'

'Why don't you two come into the caravan?' asked Daisy. 'We can discuss it over a glass of Dan's whiskey. Although we're selling water he's still got a few bottles of the real stuff there.'

They followed Daisy into the caravan. Dan and Harold were inside and greeted them with welcoming smiles.

'I expect after that speech you made, you'd like some refreshment,' said Dan.

He produced a couple of glasses with generous measures of whiskey in them. McGee and Salmon accepted the glasses.

'Your whiskey is as good as ever, Dan,' said McGee, sipping it appreciatively.

'Why do you think somebody has kidnapped the Indian girl?' demanded Daisy.

'It must be because the kidnappers think we're rich. That we've got the money to pay the bets,' said Salmon.

'How much money would that be?' asked Dan.

'Over two thousand dollars,' replied McGee.

'And how much have you got?' demanded Daisy.

'About twenty-five dollars,' replied McGee.

Daisy stared at him to decide whether he was being serious. She read enough in his face to confirm that he was indeed telling the truth. She began to laugh. She laughed so much that the effort made her double up. At last she said, wiping the tears from her eyes: 'McGee, you are priceless.'

At that moment there was a rumble of thunder. It announced the imminent arrival of something which had been missing from Stoneville for months. Rain.

'Would you believe it?' said McGee. 'If it had come a quarter of an hour earlier we would have won the bet.'

'That's all you think about, isn't it, your bet?' snapped Salmon. 'You don't care what happened to Tandolee, do you?'

'Boys! Boys! Boys!' said Dan, placatingly. 'Let's not quarrel. Let's have another drink while we watch it raining.'

Daisy poured the drinks. 'What are you going to do now, McGee?'

'If you'll come and sit on my knee I'll tell you.'

'It's all over between us. Do you understand?' she hissed.

'Yes, what are you going to do?' demanded Dan. 'If you'd like to consider it I can offer you one suggestion.'

'What's that?'

'Why don't you come back to Herford with us? You can carry on where you left off the last time you were there. You can do your sharpshooting act in the square before I start selling my whiskey. Your act always attracted the crowd.'

'At least that way the guys who placed the bets won't be able to string you up here,' chuckled Daisy.

'Hey! That's not a bad idea,' said McGee, enthusiastically.

'We can't go,' protested Salmon. 'What about Tandolee?'

Outside the caravan the groups who had set

off to find her were beginning to return. Salmon stood on the steps of the caravan and searched each group hopefully. None of them had brought Tandolee back. It was the last group that gave him some information about her.

'We came across a clearing a few miles out of town,' said a spokesman. 'A farmer who has a potato farm nearby said that some men had been camping in the clearing. They had an Indian girl with them.'

'What happened to them?' demanded Salmon, eagerly.

'They're not there now. We looked around but they've obviously high-tailed it away.'

'We could go there and find out which direction they took.' Salmon appealed to McGee.

'We'll never find which way they went. See that rain out there? It means that any tracks will be washed away.'

'McGee's right,' said Harold. 'I'm a good tracker, but with this rain I won't stand a chance of finding out which way they went.'

'There must be something we can do.' Salmon made a fist and punched the wall of the caravan in frustration.

'Get him out of here before he breaks up the caravan,' said Dan. 'There is one thing you can do though,' he added.

'What's that?' demanded Salmon, with new-found hope.

'Go and see the sheriff.'

'He won't do anything,' said McGee scornfully. 'He'll never raise a posse. Anyhow he couldn't find enough men to go with him. They've all gone back to their ranches or farms now that the rain has started.'

'You never know. He might know something about this gang. If he doesn't there's no harm in telling him that you'll be going to Herford. If he does find out anything about the gang, ask him to telegraph the sheriff there.'

'We know the sheriff of Herford. He put us in jail for a couple of days.'

'My, what an exciting life you lead, McGee,' said Daisy as she avoided the pretended punch which he aimed at her.

CHAPTER 21

Salmon hurried through the rain to the sheriff's office. Inside he found the sheriff and his deputy.

'What can I do for you?' demanded the sheriff.

'My name is Salmon. I've come to report that the Indian girl, Tandolee, is missing.'

'You're the one who rescued her from the ducking-stool,' put in the deputy.

'That's right.'

'What do you mean – missing?' demanded the sheriff. 'Do you mean she's been kidnapped, or that she's just ridden off somewhere?'

'She'd never have ridden off on her own,' averred Salmon. 'We had set up this bet about whether it would rain or not. We were due to collect the money when it rained.'

'Perhaps she collected the money herself and

went off with it,' suggested the sheriff.

'She'd never have done that,' said Salmon, hotly. 'Anyhow we lost the bet so she couldn't have collected any money.'

'You lost the bet,' said the deputy, interestedly.

'She was doing some window-shopping, while I was in a saloon. When I came out she had disappeared. I went in every shop in Main Street, but there was no sign of her. Then some of the locals said a potato farmer had seen some strangers and an Indian girl camping near his farm. When the locals reached the spot the strangers had disappeared. Of course there's no chance of tracking them now that the rain has come.'

'I don't see that we can do anything about it,' said the sheriff. 'After all, she's only an Indian.'

Salmon flared up. 'I don't see what that's got to do with it. She's a human being – the same as anybody else.'

'Why don't you have a cup of coffee,' said the deputy, diplomatically. 'Then we can discuss it further.'

While he was brewing the coffee Salmon studied the drawings on the wall. Most of them depicted outlaws with a price on their heads – the prices ranging from $100 to, in some cases, $300.

'There are a lot of outlaws here,' said Salmon,

having recovered from his outburst.

'Some of them have been on the wall for years. They're probably either in jail somewhere or other, or they will have been hanged.'

The deputy returned with the coffees. 'I see you're studying our rogues gallery.'

'Are these the latest additions to your collection?' Salmon pointed to five portraits which had been given pride of place above the others.

'That's right – they were only added to our collection a few days ago. I haven't rightly studied their names yet.'

'It says here – Finley, Stolley, Gimlet, Muller and Bling,' said Salmon, reading their names from their drawings.

'Of course it's possible that a gang of outlaws like them could have captured your Indian,' said the sheriff.

'What's happened to your partner, McGee?' demanded the deputy.

'He's on his way out to the ranch where we work – the Lazy Y.'

'Let's hope he stays on the ranch,' said the sheriff. 'We've had enough trouble with him.'

'McGee doesn't look for trouble. It just seems to find him.'

'You should know. You're his partner,' said the sheriff.

'In fact we're not stopping at the ranch. We're going to Herford.'

'Ah! Welshing on the bet, are you?' said the sheriff, with a knowing smirk.

'Certainly not,' snapped Salmon. 'We're going to Herford to perform our sharpshooters' act. With luck we should be able to get enough money to pay our bets.'

He left shortly afterwards. He had one more call to make before they left Stoneville. Ten minutes later he knocked at the familiar door.

Miss Brown opened it. 'Salmon,' she said, with a delighted smile 'It's nice to see you again. But where's Tandolee?' She ushered him into the parlour.

'That's it. I don't know.' He couldn't keep the despair out of his voice.

'The last time you both were here she said she was going window-shopping to look at the two clothes-shops in town.'

'I know. I should never have let her go on her own,' he cried.

'I was going to offer you a cup of coffee, but seeing how upset you are, I think I'll get something stronger. A whiskey, perhaps?'

She went out into the kitchen and returned with a generous quantity of whiskey in a glass.

'I never know how much of the stuff to pour,

since I'm a teetotaller myself. Is that enough?'

'More than enough,' said Salmon, with a half-smile. He sipped the whiskey appreciatively.

'I assume that you've searched everywhere for Tandolee?'

'Everywhere that I can think of. I've been in every shop and café in Stoneville.'

'What about the saloons? Oh, I forgot, she's an Indian. She wouldn't be able to go into any of the saloons.'

Salmon took another drink. 'I wonder if you could do me a favour?'

'If I can, I will.'

'My friend and I are going to Herford. We intend doing some sharpshooting to help to pay our debts.'

'Oh, yes, I forgot. You lost your bet. But only by a quarter of an hour or so.'

'If there's any news about Tandolee, could you telegraph the office in Herford. I'll call in there regularly to see whether there is any news.'

'I'd be happy to do it. I only hope nothing serious has happened to the poor girl.'

CHAPTER 22

'What are we going to do with her?' demanded Miller.

Although Tandolee was about hundred yards from the five outlaws she knew from their continued glances in her direction that they were talking about her. She was tied securely to a tree so there was no chance of her getting near enough to make out exactly what they were saying.

'There's only one thing we can do,' said Stolley. 'We'll have to get rid of her.'

'She's seen our faces,' stated Gimlet. 'We can't let her go free.'

'You mean we're going to kill her?' said a shocked Bling.

'You're getting the picture,' said Stolley.

'All right, let's get it over,' said Finley.

'Who's going to do it?' demanded Bling.

'I don't fancy it,' said Miller. 'I don't hold with killing women.'

'I've killed a few men, but I've never killed a woman,' said Gimlet. 'But if it's got to be done, it's got to be done.'

'We've beaten her half to death, now we're going to kill her,' said Bling.

'What do you suggest?' snapped Stolley. 'That we take her with us?'

'Right, let's get on with it,' said Finley, in businesslike tones. 'We'll do it the usual way. We'll draw lots.'

'Who's got matches?' demanded Gimlet.

'I have.' Bling produced a box of matches.

'Right. Count out five,' ordered Stolley. 'That is, if you can count up to five.'

Bling clumsily took out the required number of matches.

'Give them here.'

Stolley took the matches and broke one in half. He held them up to show that the broken one was hidden from view. 'All right, here are the five matches. The one who draws the short match will kill her.'

Tandolee watched the actions of the outlaws from the distance. She couldn't hear the outcome of the discussion. But when she saw Bling produce the matches, cold fear gripped her. Surely they weren't going to kill her, were they?

She could see Stolley holding up the matches. There was some hesitation as to who would be the first to choose. Eventually Bling stepped forward. She could see him choose a match. Then he held it up to show the others. However, from her distance she was unable to distinguish whether it was the short match.

The outlaws around Bling were in no doubt.

'You've chosen the short straw,' said Stolley. 'It's up to you to kill her.'

Bling looked in the direction of Tandolee.

'I'm not going to watch,' said Miller. 'I can't stand to see a woman killed.'

'We could have killed her in the first place,' said Stolley. 'We've wasted enough time with her as it is.'

'We'll get our horses and ride a short distance ahead,' said Finley. 'You shoot her and then catch us up.'

The four mounted their horses. They started to ride out of the clearing. As they passed Tandolee they all pointedly refrained from looking at her.

Tandolee watched as Bling slowly walked towards her.

'So you're the one who's going to kill me,' she

said, as he approached.

'I'm sorry I got you into this mess by giving you our names.'

'Well, it's all over now. If anyone is going to shoot me, I'd rather it would be you. You'll make it quick, won't you?'

'You don't understand, I'm not going to shoot you.'

'What do you mean?'

'As I said, I'm responsible for this mess. So I'm going to give you a chance to live.'

'You're going to set me free?' The hope in her voice almost choked her.

'Not exactly. I planned it when I tricked the others into thinking I had drawn the short match. Actually I snapped one and hid it in my hand when they weren't looking.'

'That was clever. So what are you going to do now?'

'I can't set you free because you'll get back to Stoneville before we can get on the trail.'

Tandolee's hopes sank. Here she was expecting to be set free and now Bling had stated that he wasn't going to release her.

'I'm going to leave you here,' said Bling. 'You've got a fifty-fifty chance that somebody will come along in a day or so. You're not too far off the beaten track.'

'I suppose it's better than being shot,' stated Tandolee, ungraciously.

'Exactly,' said Bling, eagerly. 'Now I'm going to fire a bullet into the air. It will make the others think I have shot you.'

He suited the deed to his words. After the sound of the shot had died away, he said, 'Good luck.'

'I'll need it,' said Tandolee.

CHAPTER 23

McGee and Salmon rode behind Dan's caravan on their way to Herford. McGee kept up a lively repartee with Daisy, who was seated on the step of the caravan. Their smiles contrasted with the glum expression on Salmon's face.

What could have happened to Tandolee? Maybe she had been kidnapped by one of her tribe. She had once mentioned a prospective husband – what was his name? No, it escaped him. Suppose this Indian had come into Stoneville to claim his future wife? Yes, it was possible. The farmer who had spotted the strangers had told the townsfolk that he was too far away to identify them. Maybe he was also too far away to see whether they were white folk or Indians. Yes, the more he thought about it the more reasonable the idea seemed.

The difficulty with that assumption was that

she wouldn't have gone away without saying goodbye to him. What had she called him when they were up on the mountain – her soul mate? He wasn't quite sure exactly what it meant. But there was no doubt that they had formed a close relationship on the mountain. A very close relationship. And he could have made it even closer if he had accepted her invitation to make love to her.

No, she would never have gone off without at least saying goodbye to him.

'Still worrying about your Indian?' chided McGee. Dan had called a halt to their progress so that they could have some coffee.

'She'd never have gone off without saying goodbye to me,' muttered Salmon to himself.

'You're a Crow Indian,' McGee addressed Henry while they were drinking their coffees. 'Do you think Tandolee would have gone away without telling Salmon that she was going?'

'No,' he replied, emphatically. 'She had been trained by the Bible folk to behave as you white folk behave. She had learned the same manners and customs as you. She would never have gone off without telling Salmon. The only reason why she wouldn't have come back is that she is dead.'

'Thank you for nothing,' snapped Salmon.

'Cheer up,' said McGee. 'When we get to

Herford we can take up our sharpshooting again. We should be able to earn some tidy money in the square. The last time we were there we did very well if I remember rightly.'

'You mean you did,' replied Salmon, with a sideways glance at Daisy.

'Salmon, if you weren't so big, I would hit you,' Daisy replied.

'It's possible that Tandolee was collected by her future husband,' said Harold, who had the irritating habit of entering the conversation when everybody else had passed on to a new subject.

'Without telling me that she had gone?' demanded Salmon.

'It all depends how close you two were,' continued Harold.

'They spent a week up on the mountain together,' stated McGee.

'Did you now,' said Daisy, regarding Salmon with new-found interest.

'We weren't that close,' he denied, vehemently.

'I hear it gets pretty cold on those mountaintops at night,' said Dan, drily.

'Nothing happened between us.' Salmon was beginning to get angry.

'Why did you go up the mountain with the

attractive Tandolee?' demanded Daisy. 'And not McGee. He was always partial to some female company if I remember rightly.'

McGee scowled at the obvious reference to his amorous nature.

'I saved Tandolee's life,' admitted Salmon, to alleviate the scrutiny of the three interested onlookers.

'How did you do that?' demanded Dan.

Salmon explained about the ducking-stool and how he had managed to turn it back upright after it had fallen on its side.

'Why did they put her in the ducking-stool?' demanded Harold.

'For the same reason that you'll end up there one day – for asking too many questions,' suggested Daisy.

'They said that she was responsible for the drought,' stated McGee.

'What a lot of rubbish,' said Harold, beginning to get angry. 'How could she be responsible for the drought.'

'They said her father was a witch-doctor. That she came from generations of witches,' said McGee.

'They put her in the ducking-stool because she is an Indian,' snapped Harold. He pulled his blanket around him, signifying that he didn't intend taking any further part in the discussion.

'I remember seeing that ducking-stool,' reminisced Daisy. 'It was in the church in Stoneville. It gave a list of the kind of people who were ducked when it was used in England. Among them were thieves, vagabonds and scolding wives. There was one thing it missed out though. It didn't say deceitful men.'

'You wait until we get to Herford, young lady,' said McGee, pretending it was a serious threat.

'I think it's about time we were on our way,' said Dan, diplomatically.

CHAPTER 24

'Oh, my God!'

Miss Brown didn't usually resort to blaspheming but on this occasion it was more than justified. She had opened her front to a timid knock. In fact the knock had been so quiet that she almost thought she had imagined it. However she had decided to make sure, since it could have been one of the children who lived near by. Their mother was always running out of provisions, eggs, sugar, milk and even bread. On such occasions she would send one of her brood (she had seven or eight children) to ask Miss Brown whether she could borrow the required commodity. She knew that Miss Brown, being a good neighbour, would invariably accede to the request.

But the sight that presented itself on the doorstep was not one of the neighbour's children. It was a bedraggled figure who, if it hadn't been for the colour of her skin, Miss Brown would in all probability not have recognized. It was Tandolee. She was hanging on to the doorpost and displaying every possibility that when she released it she would collapse.

'Oh, my dear, what's happened to you?' Miss Brown put her arm around her and led her gingerly into the parlour.

Tandolee sank gratefully into the armchair.

'I never thought I would sit in a chair again,' she said. She had held back any traces of feeling as a sign of weakness when she had been beaten. She had even managed to betray no signs of emotion when she had discovered that she was going to be shot. But now just the mere physical act of sinking back in an armchair proved too much for her. She burst into tears. Soon she was crying as though she would never stop.

'That's it, have a good cry, my dear. My mother always said it was one of the best of nature's cures.'

Several minutes later, when Tandolee's sobbing had at last ceased and Miss Brown had brought in two cups of coffee, she ventured to voice the question she had been burning to utter since Tandolee's appearance.

'What happened to you?'

Tandolee, having got the immediate emotion out of her system, was able to relate her account in a calm voice. Miss Brown did not interrupt. But it was obvious, from her change of expression from surprise to shock and then to horror, what effect her tale was having on her.

When Tandolee had finished, Miss Brown said: 'You'll have to go to the sheriff with your tale.'

'What, like this?' Tandolee managed a half-smile. Her clothes were hanging in shreds as a result of the beating from Finley's belt.

'I'll fix a bath for you. Then I've got another dress that my niece left here. I assume you can bath after the beating you had?'

'Yes, I made them rub salt in the wounds. Then later the rain helped to cool them. It was the one benefit from the rain.'

'You poor dear. I'll see about the bath while you're finishing your coffee.'

In fact when Miss Brown returned Tandolee was curled up in the chair, fast asleep. Miss Brown was on the point of waking her then she changed her mind. She went over to a writing-desk. She took out a sheet of notepaper and wrote a message on it. She left the message in a prominent place on the writing-desk. Then, after collecting her coat and pinning on her hat

149

she went out, closing the door carefully behind her in order not to wake her sleeping guest.

When Miss Brown returned an hour or so later, Tandolee was still asleep. Miss Brown gently shook her until she awoke.

'I'm sorry I went to sleep,' said Tandolee, rubbing her eyes.

'I doesn't matter. While you were asleep I went to the telegraph office. I had promised Salmon that I would send a telegraph to the office in Herford if 1 had any news about you. I sent him a telegram saying you were safe and well. At least half of it is true, since you are safe, although you haven't recovered fully from your ordeal.'

Tandolee smiled. 'I'm sure I'll recover quite quickly. We Crow Indians are a hardy lot.'

'The other thing is, I went to see the sheriff. I had to call to see him before he closed his office. I told him exactly everything you told me. How you had been beaten half to death, how you had been left for dead by the outlaws and how a prospector had found you tied to the tree and brought you in to me.'

'What did the sheriff say?'

'I gave him some of the names of the outlaws, Finley and Stolley and Bling. By a strange coincidence he had their pictures on the wall, It seems they are wanted in several states for their activities as bank-robbers. So he also has sent a telegram to Herford. To the sheriff this time, telling him that the gang are on their way there. I hope I did the right thing.'

'Miss Brown, you are an angel.' Tandolee hugged her.

After a while Miss Brown said: 'I think you had better let me go, or I'll start crying too. '

Tandolee had her bath. Since it was getting late, Miss Brown loaned her a dressing-gown.

'There, that will do until tomorrow. I'm afraid you'll have to get up early.'

'Why must I do that?' demanded a puzzled Tandolee.

'Because I've got one more surprise for you. I've booked you a seat on the stage tomorrow. It only goes twice a week to Herford. And tomorrow is one of the days. I guessed you'd like to make sure that Salmon is also safe.'

The square in Herford was fairly crowded. It was a large square by Western standards, since most towns didn't have the huge squares that the cities and towns in Europe boasted. In one corner Dan had parked his caravan. Daisy and Henry stood nearby while Dan began his speech.

'Gather round if you want to taste the nectar

of the gods – the best drink this side of the Elysian Fields.'

'Where's the Elysian Fields?' enquired an onlooker.

'I'm not quite sure. But after you've tasted my whiskey, you won't want to bother about them anyhow, or anything else for that matter. All your troubles will have vanished. But before I introduce you to the delights of my whiskey I have a surprise for you. Some of you may remember that a few months ago we staged a sharpshooter's exhibition for your entertainment. Well, I'm delighted to say that, at great expense, we have managed to persuade McGee and Salmon to return and perform their act just for your benefit. Ladies and gentlemen, I give you McGee and Salmon.'

McGee and Salmon were dressed in their usual shirt and jeans, the only difference in their appearance was that McGee was wearing a white Stetson, while Salmon was wearing a black one.

The two arranged a clear corridor between them for their act. The crowd obligingly spread out to give them room. Those who hadn't seen their act on the previous occasion looked on interestedly, particularly five of the crowd named Finley, Stolley, Miller, Gimblet and Bling.

The sharpshooters were finally satisfied with

the distribution of the crowd. They went into their act. It consisted at first of hurling insults at each other. Some of the comments were quite funny and they had the audience in fits of laughter. Eventually, when the insults came to an end, they stood back to back. They began to walk away from each other while McGee was counting the number of paces.

At that moment someone burst forward from the crowd.

'Look out, Salmon,' shouted Tandolee.

Salmon's quick glance took in the fact that five men with drawn guns were facing him. His reaction was instantaneous. He flung himself flat on the ground. The sound of gunfire echoed around the square. McGee, who had been walking in the direction away from Salmon, had turned at the sound of Tandolee's warning. He too was now lying on the ground.

The five outlaws hadn't been able to claim any success with their first round of fire, and they were finding it increasingly difficult to follow the initial shots, since their targets were lying on the ground about a hundred yards away and firing back at them. In fact the only successes in the gun-battle belonged to Salmon and McGee. Both had been successful with their shots. The result was that now instead of facing five gunmen they were now facing three – Finley, Stolley and Gimlet.

Finley, realizing that the battle wasn't going their way, changed its course. He dived across to where Tandolee was standing, and before she realized what was happening, he grabbed her. He held her in front of him. McGee and Salmon, seeing the threat that one of their bullets might hit Tandolee, stopped firing.

'That's right, Salmon,' shouted Finley. 'If you value your girlfriend's life you had better throw your guns away.'

Tandolee was struggling in his arms.

'Don't listen to him, Salmon,' she cried. 'If you throw your guns away he'll kill you.'

'I'm going to count up to three,' said Finley. 'If you don't throw your guns away, I'll kill this bitch. One. . . .'

Tandolee was intensifying her struggle. Salmon and McGee were clearly undecided what course of action to follow.

'Two. . . .'

At that moment Tandolee succeeded in her objective. Finley was holding her with one arm while trying to hold his revolver in his other hand. Tandolee managed to turn her body, forcing Finley to turn with her. Too late he realized that he was now presenting the sharpshooters with, if not a full target, at least half of one. McGee and Salmon didn't need a second invitation. They both put bullets into him.

Stolley, being a firm believer that discretion was the better part of valour, disappeared into the crowd. Gimlet was undecided whether he, too, should try to flee. He was stopped in his tracks by Tandolee's voice.

'Are you going to run away too, Gimlet?'

He spun round. She was standing where Finley had fallen. Unbelievably she was holding Finley's gun in her hand, which she had snatched up from the corpse.

Seeing Tandolee standing with the gun not too far away, Gimlet raised his revolver to aim at her. McGee and Salmon were watching the scene. McGee raised his own gun to fire at Gimlet but Salmon put a restraining hand on his arm. 'The distance is too far.'

'You bitch! You caused all the trouble,' spat out Gimlet.

He raised his gun, but before he could shoot Tanadlee had fired. The bullet hit him in the head and splattered his brains over the sidewalk.

'You always said to aim for the head, didn't you, Gimlet,' she stated, calmly.

Some time later eight people were squeezed into

the sheriff's office. The only person whom the sheriff and his deputy hadn't met before was Tandolee. McGee and Salmon had just finished describing the events which had ended with the four outlaws being shot.

'Tandolee shot the last outlaw,' Salmon enthused. 'It was a great shot.'

'I've never known an Indian who could shoot,' said the sheriff.

'Salmon taught me to shoot when we were up on the mountain together,' supplied Tandolee.

'I see,' said the sheriff, casting an interested eye at Salmon.

'It's a long story,' said Salmon.

McGee was studying the rogues gallery.

'The four outlaws are here,' he exclaimed. 'There are bounties on all of them. I've added it up and it will come to one thousand dollars.'

'That should go towards helping to pay the bets you owe in Stoneville,' said Dan.

'We owe over two thousand dollars.'

'You could pay, say, half the bet. After all, the rain was only a few minutes late.'

'Hold on,' said Salmon. 'The bounty for killing Gimlet is owed to Tandolee. That's three hundred dollars.'

'I do not want the money,' said Tandolee. 'It's yours. You can do what you like with it.'

'She's repaid the debt,' explained Harold. 'You saved her life, she helped to kill the outlaws.' He retired into the corner after what was, for him, a long speech.

'What's this about you three claiming you were responsible for bringing the rain to Stoneville?' demanded the deputy.

'It's a long story,' said McGee. 'If you'll come and watch our sharpshooting act, we'll tell you about it after the event.'

'And over a glass of my whiskey,' said Dan.

WOLVERHAMPTON
LIBRARIES